"I never tho[...]
much as I misse[...]
know I haven't [...]
but . . . well, now you kno[...]

"I understand," Elizabeth answered quaveringly. For a moment Ryan gripped her around the waist so tightly it almost hurt; he let go and gently cupped her face instead. Elizabeth sighed in sweet relief. She felt his breath on her lips as he brought his face closer to hers. The tips of their noses just barely touched.

"Oh, Liz," Ryan murmured. "You're really here."

"Yes, Ryan. I'm here."

Finally Ryan's mouth met hers, first tenderly, then passionately. She was instantly lost, her head swimming and heart thudding against her chest; the world seemed to disappear when Ryan rained silken kisses all over her face. Then Ryan's lips found hers again. He and Elizabeth clung to each other for what seemed an eternity, until finally they broke apart, gasping for air. The only other sound was the roaring of the ocean, the waves crashing in time with their breaths.

SWEET VALLEY
UNIVERSITY®

Originally published in USA by Bantam Books

First publication in Great Britain

PRINTING HISTORY
Bantam edition published 1998

Beauty and the Beach

Written by
Laurie John

Created by
FRANCINE PASCAL

BANTAM BOOKS
NEW YORK · TORONTO · LONDON · SYDNEY · AUCKLAND

To Thomas John Pascal Wenk

Chapter One

It won't be long now, Elizabeth Wakefield thought nervously. Her heart thumped hard against her chest; her hands were so hot and slippery, they could barely clutch the steering wheel. A brisk sea breeze blew through the open windows but did little to cool her flushed face as she drove down the nearly deserted freeway. *I could be seeing him in less than an hour. But I'm not ready . . . not yet.*

Since they'd missed the Thursday evening rush hour, the Wakefield twins and Nina Harper were making amazingly good time. Even though it was the second week in June, the roads were surprisingly free of vacation traffic. All in all, it was smooth sailing. But when a white convertible whizzed past the Jeep, a glimpse of the driver's wavy brown hair made

Elizabeth's stomach do an extra somersault.

Of course that wasn't him, Elizabeth told herself as she adjusted her grip on the wheel. *You've got to get hold of yourself. Concentrate on the beautiful sunset, concentrate on the gorgeous coastal view—concentrate on anything but Ryan Taylor.*

That wasn't easy to do. Ryan Taylor, the brooding, dedicated, and utterly gorgeous head lifeguard who had won Elizabeth's heart the summer before, wasn't a guy you could easily ignore. She and Ryan had each gone their separate ways at the end of the summer, and now Elizabeth was returning to Sweet Valley Shore to lifeguard once again. Whether or not the two of them would pick up where they left off was anyone's guess. Frustrated, Elizabeth stifled a groan and pressed down on the accelerator, urging the Jeep down the last few miles of the freeway toward their destination.

"All right, Liz!" Jessica Wakefield crowed from the backseat. "Now we're cruising. Sweet Valley Shore, here we come!"

Almost instinctively Elizabeth eased up on the gas pedal. After all, it was up to her to be the responsible Wakefield twin. Even though she and Jessica looked identical, they were opposites in virtually every way. Jessica was an impulsive, fun-loving free spirit, while Elizabeth was far more studious and levelheaded. At Sweet Valley University, where they were both freshmen, Elizabeth could often be found working at the campus TV station or in the library while Jessica was either hanging out with her sorority sisters at the Theta Alpha Theta house or off campus at the nearest mall.

"All you foxy guys better look out!" Jessica shouted to no one in particular. "The babe patrol is closing in, and we're ready to line you up and read you your rights!"

A loud, exasperated sigh erupted from the passenger seat. "*Excuse* me, Jessica." Nina Harper groaned. "We're going to the beach to *bay* watch, not *babe* watch."

"Sooo, Nina, does that mean Paul Jackson's off-limits this summer?" Jessica teased.

Nina had told Elizabeth all about how she had been uncontrollably attracted to Paul Jackson the previous summer; the fact that he worked on the rival South Beach Squad made him seem deliciously forbidden. But he was mysterious too; at one point Nina had actually suspected Paul of committing a series of break-ins *and* sabotaging the Sweet Valley Shore Squad so that South Beach would win the merit-pay contest at summer's end. But to Nina's relief, Paul had turned out to be working undercover for the sheriff's department; his

3

squadmate, Rachel Max, had been the trouble-maker.

"Absolutely," Nina replied, her voice chilly. "Paul's been busy at the police academy, and that's fine by me. I'm on a strict man-free diet, and I intend on sticking to it."

Elizabeth winced and bit her lip. She was so dazed from thinking about Ryan that she had almost forgotten how guys were a sore subject with Nina at the moment. Silently Elizabeth prayed that Jessica wouldn't pursue the subject.

"How *boring!*" Jessica cried. "Don't tell me you actually plan on being *faithful* to Bryan this summer. Just think of all the hunks you'll miss out on!"

For a second Elizabeth actually wondered if it would be possible to hide under the dashboard and drive at the same time.

"'Faithful' and 'Bryan' don't belong in the same sentence," Nina snarled, her usually warm brown eyes turning cold. "And I'm not going near any so-called hunks this summer—not unless I've got a muzzle and a leash handy."

"Nina—," Elizabeth cautioned.

"What's your point?" Jessica asked in apparent fascination.

"My point is, all men are *dogs,*" Nina shot over her shoulder. "Oh, wait—I take that back. Dogs, at least, are faithful."

4

Jessica's mouth hung open for a moment. "Jeez! What's gotten into *you*?"

"Uh, look," Elizabeth began hesitantly. "I don't think—"

"Oh no, I *do* think," Nina insisted, holding one hand up in front of her as if she were trying to stop an oncoming car. "I believe it's time I let Jessica in on the sad, sad truth about Bryan Nelson."

"Bryan?" Jessica exclaimed, her blue-green eyes wide and expectant. "What, did your boyfriend do something stupid?"

"Stupid?" Nina cried indignantly. "Stupid doesn't even begin to describe it. I'll sum it up for you as briefly as possible. You know how Bryan is interning on Capitol Hill again this summer?"

"Uh-huh," Jessica breathed.

"Well, I called Bryan, the man to whom I have devoted entire *months* of my life, last night just to remind him that I was leaving for the beach today. And do you know what he said?"

"What?"

"*Nothing*, that's what. Because after six tries and no answer a syrupy, sexy, *female* voice finally answered his phone!"

"No!" Jessica covered her mouth in shock.

"There has to be an explanation, Nina," Elizabeth offered. "Maybe that girl in Bryan's room was a fellow aide. They were probably just working on a project together."

"What kind of 'project' could they have been working on at one in the morning?" Nina scoffed. "You should have heard how breathy she sounded. I mean, come on, what would *you* do in this situation?"

"I'd be ready to strangle him," Jessica said.

"I'd be pretty upset," Elizabeth admitted. "But I still think you should have given Bryan a chance to explain instead of just hanging up on him like you did."

"What could Bryan possibly say that I'd want to listen to?" Nina retorted. "Men always lie when they're cornered."

Elizabeth slumped in her seat. It was obviously useless to try to cheer Nina up. She remained silent as she watched the sun begin its slow descent. A stunning array of colors—pinks, blues, oranges, even a deep violet—streaked across the sky. But Elizabeth decided against pointing it out; she figured the gorgeous scene would have no effect on the sour mood in the Jeep.

"So Jessica, what about you?" Nina asked, breaking a long silence. "Are you counting on a certain blue-eyed hound dog from the University of Chicago to be anxiously awaiting your arrival?"

"I'm not just counting on it, Nina. I *know*

it," Jessica replied confidently. "And Ben Mercer is no dog, I can guarantee that. He must be flipping out, wondering when I'm going to get there so he can give me the kiss of a lifetime."

"Does anyone know if he's going to be living with us again this summer?" Elizabeth asked cautiously.

"I sure don't," Nina snarled. "And I sure don't *care* either. The fewer men in our house, the better."

After a brief silence Elizabeth looked in the rearview mirror and caught Jessica chewing nervously on her cuticle. "Jess? Do you know if Ben is going to be living with us?"

"Ummm . . . Ben hasn't exactly told me where he's staying," Jessica admitted.

Nina snorted derisively. "Is he even going to *be* there this summer?"

"Well, of course!" Jessica insisted. "He wouldn't miss out on a chance to spend a whole summer with *me*. Are you *kidding*?"

Nina groaned and rolled her eyes, but Elizabeth held her tongue. Jessica wasn't fooling her a bit with her big brave act. Elizabeth knew all too well that Jessica had stopped writing and calling Ben Mercer months ago. Now Jessica was terrified that he'd be angry at her for leaving him hanging after their heated summer romance. In fact, Jessica was *so* anxious, she was

7

even half hoping Ben might not show up at all. *Now she's trying to convince herself that she has nothing to be afraid of—that she and Ben can pick up where they left off,* Elizabeth realized sympathetically. *Just like I'm trying to convince myself about Ryan.*

"So you're not upset that Ben never transferred to UCLA?" Nina asked, a smirk of disbelief on her face.

"Not at all," Jessica answered briskly. "I'm sure Ben has a perfectly good explanation. Some emergency must have kept him at the U of C—some big, secret chemistry project for the government or something. Anyway, you know what they say, 'Absence makes the heart grow fonder.'"

They also say, "Out of sight, out of mind," Elizabeth added silently. *I hope we're not both setting ourselves up for a fall.*

"Yes!" Jessica cried as the three-story Victorian beach house came into view. "Here it is, ladies—our home away from home!"

Memories crowded in Elizabeth's mind as she steered the Jeep into the driveway. A lump grew in her throat when she noticed the dotted curtains billowing from a second-floor window on the ocean side. *There's my old room,* she thought mistily as she turned off the ignition.

8

While Jessica and Nina piled out of the Jeep and began unloading their bags, Elizabeth watched them blankly, hardly believing where she was. *I'm back,* she told herself. *I'm really back at Sweet Valley Shore.*

"Think you brought enough stuff with you, Jessica?" Nina asked sarcastically as she strode toward the house, her two duffel bags over her strong shoulders. Jessica was in the process of dragging all five of her overloaded suitcases out onto the lawn.

To shut it all out, Elizabeth leaned back and closed her eyes. She breathed in the salty sea air and listened to the roar of the nearby ocean. The smell, the sounds all reminded her of that night last summer when she and Ryan first kissed. His lips had been so strong, so sure. She had melted into his arms, unable to stop herself from giving in—

"Hel-*lo*-o!"

A sudden, insistent tap on Elizabeth's shoulder brought her back to the present.

"Are you coming out or not?" Jessica asked, suitcase in hand.

Elizabeth blinked twice. "What?"

"Jeez, Liz, are you waiting for *us* to carry *you* inside? Or maybe you're waiting for *Ryan*."

"Really, Jess, grow up!" Elizabeth felt her face burn a little. "I was just reminiscing, if you

9

don't mind." She jumped out of the Jeep and grabbed her two small suitcases out of the back.

Jessica chuckled. "I don't mind, and I don't think Ryan will either. I bet he's just as excited about seeing you as Ben is about seeing me."

I'm doomed, then, Elizabeth thought. With a wistful sigh Elizabeth followed Jessica into the house and trudged up the stairs to the second floor.

"Cool, Liz! My old room is still free," Jessica crowed excitedly from the third floor.

Elizabeth nodded absentmindedly, walked into her old room, and shut the door behind her. She dumped her bags onto the floor and stood for a long moment, gazing blankly around at the cozy surroundings—the same friendly rose-patterned wallpaper and hooked rugs. Elizabeth smoothed down the quilt on the bed and wandered over to the window. Outside, the ocean shimmered and glistened under the early evening sky like dark, mottled glass. The waves rolled and crashed against the beach in a hypnotic rhythm. Some of the tightness in Elizabeth's muscles began to ease.

I wish I could be as self-assured as Jessica, she thought. *But it's so hard to know where I stand when it comes to Ryan. He can be so moody and erratic. Maybe he* has *forgotten all about me, despite our wonderful summer together.*

10

She remembered the few conversations she'd had with Ryan since summer had ended. They'd been pleasant enough, but Ryan had made it clear that he wasn't the type of guy who enjoyed talking on the phone. *Maybe* you *should forget all about* him, her conscience told her.

No, she answered silently. *Ryan Taylor isn't someone you just "forget." Once you've met him, the memory sticks with you—forever.*

With another sigh Elizabeth turned away from the window. The past sensation of Ryan's firm, warm mouth claiming her own made her close her eyes and shiver.

You're losing it, Liz, she told herself, snapping back to reality. *You're driving yourself crazy*.

Elizabeth took a cursory glance at her suitcases and decided she could unpack later. What she needed now was to get out and get some fresh air before she suffocated on the memory of Ryan Taylor.

"I can't believe this, Jessica," Nina said as she freed her ten-speed from the back of the Jeep. "You swore you were going to pack light this time."

"I only packed the essentials."

"'Essentials,'" Nina echoed, glaring at the mound of suitcases littering the front lawn.

"Mm-hmm," Jessica confirmed. "As you can

11

see, it's hardly *anything*. I don't think I can make it through the summer on so little."

Shaking her head, Nina walked her bike over to the nearest tree. *Jessica Wakefield never ceases to amaze me,* she thought.

"Um, Nina," Jessica began sweetly, "could you help me with one or two or three of these bags? Pretty please?"

With a groan Nina stormed over to the pile of luggage. *Unbelievable,* she thought. *But Jessica is certainly predictable.*

Nina picked up two bags and staggered under the weight. "Just this once," she croaked. "If you weren't Liz's sister, you could forget it."

"Well, lucky me, then," Jessica chirped as she picked up two smaller bags. "Just think of this as pretraining. Lifeguards have to be in peak condition, you know. Carrying my luggage—especially *those* two bags—is a lot like weight lifting."

"Very funny," Nina grumbled. When she saw Jessica having trouble getting the door open, Nina dropped one of the bags and helped her.

I know that Jessica is a lot stronger than she looks, Nina thought, irritated, *but why does she choose to perpetuate the helpless-female stereotype? It's women like her that encourage men to treat us so condescendingly.*

"Thanks, Nina. Too bad there are no strong, sexy guys to help us carry these bags."

"We don't need *any* guys to help us," Nina fumed. "*I* don't anyway."

"*Bzzzzz*—sorry, wrong answer," Jessica declared as she stepped into the living room. "I think a guy is *exactly* what you need right now. A fling with a sexy hunk is the perfect cure for what ails you."

"I'd rather take two aspirin and call you in the morning, Dr. Jessica," Nina said flatly, setting down Jessica's suitcases and massaging her own shoulders. Even though Nina was in top physical condition, her muscles were protesting.

"Can you help me get them upstairs to my room?" Jessica coaxed. "I'd be *reeeally* grateful." Smiling sweetly, she picked up her smaller bags and skipped upstairs.

Nina stared at Jessica's back for an awestruck moment. "The girl has nerve, I'll give her that," she muttered, looking down at the bags and imagining them as some sort of hot new exercise regimen: The Three-Story Luggage Sprint. Exhaling sharply, she squatted, picked up the bags, and began her ascent. But she nearly tripped on the third stair.

"C'mon, Nina," Jessica called over her shoulder impatiently. "What's taking you so long?"

Briefly Nina considered homicide. But in the end she decided against it—she was too beat. After she struggled to the second-floor landing,

13

Nina had to lean against the wall and gasp for air.

Looking the very picture of elegance, Jessica posed against the third-floor banister and shook her head. "Such a shame, Nina. You're out of shape." Jessica smiled knowingly. "A hot little romance with the right guy would turn your life around."

"For the last time, Jessica," Nina said through gritted teeth, "I am *not* interested in meeting men. I happen to be allergic to dogs, in case you didn't know."

Jessica came down the stairs and grabbed one of the bags. "Too bad, so sad," she quipped as she dragged the suitcase up the stairs behind her.

"I'm totally serious. I'm *not* going to have time for fun and games. I'm here to do my job and improve myself." Nina shoved the last bag into Jessica's room and slumped against the doorway, panting. *I'll do whatever it takes,* she added silently, *to put Bryan Nelson and the entire male population out of my mind.*

"So if a totally babelicious guy were to ask you out, you'd say no," Jessica taunted.

"That's right," Nina said firmly. "'Babelicious' is only one side of the coin. It takes a lot more than good looks to make a guy perfect—it takes good character too. Therefore, perfect men do *not* exist."

"But what if one did?" Jessica pushed on. "Let's say he was tall—"

14

"Six-foot three," Nina amended. "That's the ideal height."

"And what if he had great pecs—"

"Calves," Nina responded before she could stop herself. "Mmm. Really ripped-looking calves . . . and"—her eyes narrowed—"a killer smile. Nice teeth—nice teeth are key. And he'd have to be the bohemian type—"

"No preppies for you, right?"

"—and have . . . a *tattoo*. Yeah, a tattoo—a small one. He'd have a laid-back, sweet personality with absolutely *no* interest in rabble-rousing or throwing himself into political causes."

Nina took a deep breath as unwanted images of Bryan campaigning at the Black Student Union suddenly rose in her mind. "My perfect guy wouldn't *dream* of being an activist," Nina added forcefully. "He'd put me first—*always*." As her last words echoed in the room Nina realized her heart was pounding fast—a little *too* fast.

Jessica kicked a suitcase out of her way and dropped down onto her bed. "So what you're saying—"

"So what I'm saying is he'd have to be the opposite of Bryan," Nina practically shouted. "The *complete* opposite!"

"OK! OK! I get the picture," Jessica insisted, holding up both hands in front of her.

15

But Nina couldn't stop. No matter how hard she tried, Nina couldn't push back the surge of red-hot anger inside her. "What I'm looking for, Jessica, is a rare specimen—a totally faithful man," Nina declared breathlessly, spinning around and running toward the stairs. "Which means he'd have to live on a deserted island— with me being the only woman around for miles!"

Whew, at least I'm better off than Nina, Jessica reassured herself as she dove into her largest suitcase. *I'm not totally paranoid about men. I know there are nice, loyal guys around. I just hope—I mean, I just* know *that Ben is one of them.*

In the midst of burrowing through shirts, dresses, and shorts Jessica stopped and held up a yellow T-shirt dress. *Perfect,* she thought. *Casual, but sexy.* Swiftly she yanked off her clothes and changed into the dress. But she was surprised to discover that her heart was fluttering madly against her rib cage and her hands were shaking.

Calm down, she warned herself. *You have to find out if Ben's in the house. Maybe he is, maybe he isn't. But you still have to make sure you look good first.*

"OK, now where did I pack my round

brush?" Jessica wondered as she began tearing through her other bags. Clothes, magazines, and shoes burst out and scattered all over the floor. Bottles and jars exploded from her makeup tote. In a matter of minutes the whole place looked as if a twister had hit it.

"*Aaargh!*" she screamed in exasperation. "Didn't I bring *anything* that I *needed?*"

After a long struggle Jessica located her brush and gave herself a quick twenty strokes. Then she tracked down her favorite new lip gloss and natural-look eye shadow, giving herself frantic dabs of each. When she was finished, Jessica took one look at her reflection and calmed down considerably.

That's more like it, she told herself. *Liz may enjoy going around looking like Nature Girl, but I know sophisticated guys like Ben prefer a woman who* cultivates *her beauty.*

Despite her casual-but-sexy appearance, Jessica's knees were knocking as she inched her way down the two flights of stairs.

I wonder if he's living here, Jessica thought. *In fact, I wonder if he's going to be here this summer at all. Maybe I'm just getting freaked out over nothing.*

When she reached the door of the room Ben had lived in the previous summer, her heart thudded so loudly, she was surprised the whole

17

house didn't shake. With a trembling fist she timidly knocked on the door. Total silence. Jessica knocked again, this time louder. No answer. Jessica hesitated, then turned the knob. The door opened, and she peered inside.

A University of Chicago sweatshirt lay draped over a chair.

The faint aroma of lime cologne hung in the air.

Ben.

Her heart in her throat, Jessica slammed the door shut and backed away as if she'd seen a ghost.

I have seen a ghost, she realized. *The ghost of summer romances past—and I'm living with him!*

Her mouth dry as cotton, Jessica stumbled toward the staircase and tore up the two flights of stairs to her room. *Omigosh!* she thought, hurling herself onto her bed. *Ben's here. He's really here! But . . . but where is he?*

"He must be out," Jessica answered herself. "Maybe he's buying me a huge welcome bouquet of roses or something." But what was she supposed to do while she waited for him to show up?

Jessica lay frozen for a second until her gaze fell on the horrible mess around her. Her pink cotton minidress was in the wastebasket, and her most expensive sweater was wedged under the desk. Her favorite T-shirt was half out the open window. Jessica jumped up from her bed and yanked the shirt from the windowsill, pausing for a second to drink in the soothing view.

Unpacking will keep my mind occupied, she realized, carefully hanging up her dress. Walking back over to her suitcases, Jessica stumbled over a pair of shoes and banged into the dresser. One of the drawers sprang open and crashed to the floor. Face flushed, she stooped to shove the drawer back into place and knocked her elbow into the closet. It made a resounding booming noise, which was quickly followed by the sound of a downstairs door slamming loudly.

"He's back," she gasped. "That *must* be him." She whirled around and stared at the door as if the magnificent shoulders and killer smile of Ben Mercer were about to magically appear there.

Don't be an idiot, she chastised herself. *How would Ben even know you're up here?* But when she heard footsteps moving up the stairs, her heart began thumping triple time. And when she heard a light tap on her door, her spine tingled dangerously.

"C-Come in," Jessica stammered.

"Hey, Jess."

Ben Mercer's trim, muscular frame seemed to fill the entire doorway as he cautiously stepped into her room. He wore baggy khaki shorts, Birkenstock sandals, and a form-fitting yellow tank top that fit his form perfectly. The color of his shirt made his tan look extra rich and dark; it accentuated the electric blue of his eyes and the whiteness of his teeth. When Jessica remembered the washboard abs that now lay concealed beneath that tank top, she nearly passed out.

"How's it going, hot stuff?" Ben asked, smiling sheepishly.

Chapter Two

"H-Hi, Ben," Jessica sputtered, amazed that she was able to choke out not only one whole word, but two.

"I thought it was you up here," he said lightly. "I knew it when I heard all that crashing around. Either that or we've got an ultraclumsy mouse somewhere, Blondie."

Hearing that nickname again—the same nickname Jessica had found so horribly annoying at the beginning of the previous summer—sent relief and confidence flowing through her veins.

Of course *Ben couldn't bear to stay away from me,* Jessica thought with pride. *As soon as he knew I was up here, he had to come running. He couldn't even wait one minute!*

Fluttering her lashes, Jessica stooped gracefully

to pick up a silvery one-piece. "It's good to see you can still hit those high marks on the BBWI," she purred.

Ben looked confused for a moment, then laughed easily and ran his hand through his thick, dark hair. "Oh yeah." He chuckled. "I almost forgot about the Ben's Biting Wit Index."

Beaming, Jessica reached inside her closet and fumbled for a clothes hanger, but it slipped from her excited fingers. Ben scooped up the hanger and took the swimsuit from her, hanging it neatly and sliding it into the closet. "Still the same butterfingers, I see. Hard to believe those same hands can save lives." He pulled the sliding closet doors shut and stepped back toward the doorway.

Jessica pushed back a twinge of annoyance. Ben could be so sarcastic sometimes—*most* of the time. But when he flashed her his flawless, blinding grin, her heart instantly melted.

"You look like you've taken good care of yourself, Mercer," she quipped. "But let me guess—you still spend all your free time thinking deep, deep thoughts."

Ben leaned against the door and crossed his arms. "You look good too, Blondie. But let *me* guess—you've been spending all your free time doing anything *but* think."

Jessica snorted. "You haven't changed a bit," she shot back flirtatiously. "Still taking cheap shots when you have nothing original to say. Anyway, I thought that's what you liked about me—the fact that I'm not some boring old egghead like you."

"Is that what you think?" he asked softly.

"Yup." Jessica sidled even closer and stroked Ben's muscular, tanned forearm. The atmosphere was so charged that she could feel goose bumps erupt on her skin. *He's trying to act so cool, but I know the truth,* Jessica crowed to herself. *He's probably shaking in his sandals.*

She looked up into his hypnotic blue eyes. "How long have you been here?"

"About a week. I came down early to help a friend get through tryouts."

"You'd make a great coach," Jessica breathed, a seductive smile curving her lips. "Your friend is lucky. Did he make the squad?"

"My friend?" Ben repeated as if he were trying to shake himself out of a trance. "Oh yeah, my friend made it." He suddenly stepped back and rubbed his forehead—the heat of their attraction was obviously getting the best of him. "Hey, you know, it's been a long day," he said hastily. "I'm dying for a little sleep. And besides, if *you're* going to finish unpacking, I'd better clear out. You need all the space you can get."

Jessica stuck out her tongue. "Very funny. I'll see you in the morning, OK?"

With a curious gleam in his eye Ben raised one brow and turned toward the stairs. "Sure, Blondie." He gave her a quick wave before disappearing over the landing.

Jessica stood smiling for a second before she shut the door. Facing the mirror, she grabbed a raspberry crop top and held it under her chin. *Ben loves me in pink,* she thought giddily. *Let's face it. Ben loves me, period.*

As she dropped the shirt on the floor Jessica wondered why she ever had a reason to be worried about their reunion in the first place. *Ben's not mad at me at all,* she realized. *In fact, he totally wants me!*

Flopping down on her bed, Jessica hugged herself. This was going to be even easier than she thought! *Just call me Queen Midas,* she thought triumphantly. *Everything I touch turns to gold.*

Elizabeth . . . Elizabeth . . . The dark, inky waves seemed to beckon as they rolled and crashed against the sand. *Alone, alone,* a passing seagull seemed to moan as it swooped above her. Its mournful cry harmonized perfectly with the ocean's soft lament. The beach was so lonely and desolate, Elizabeth felt as if she were the last human on earth.

So far the walk on the beach had worked wonders

on Elizabeth's stressed-out body. The knotted muscles in her back and legs had begun to unclench as soon as she made her way across the dunes. She had taken off her tennis shoes and rolled up the cuffs of her chinos. She had smiled as the silky sand caressed her toes. She had felt as if all her physical tension had been carried away on the soft breeze wafting in from the sea.

Her peace of mind was another story entirely.

Isn't this what you wanted? she asked herself as she dug a toe into wet sand. *A little solitude? A chance to think? Then how come you're not satisfied?*

Biting her lip, she walked faster down the beach, stopping only to throw a stone into the ocean. *Admit it. You didn't* really *want to be alone tonight. You were hoping that—*

Elizabeth stopped herself. She was being incredibly foolish. Hoping for something didn't necessarily make it happen—or make it good.

The huge, full moon drenched the dunes and deep, dark ocean in cool silver, and Elizabeth shivered. *I should have brought a sweater,* she realized, rubbing her arms vigorously. The surf looked black and cold as it foamed against the sand. *It sure is getting chilly out here.*

"Elizabeth!"

The ocean can't really be calling my name, she thought wildly as she whirled around. As if it

25

were a mirage, Elizabeth stood transfixed as she saw the figure of a man running across the sand toward her. He drew closer, and her heart seemed to slow down, then stop. *Could it be . . .*

"Hey, Liz, is that you?" the man called, his tall, powerful figure looming closer. In the moonlight Elizabeth could barely make out that his wide shoulders were clad in a T-shirt, his narrow hips in Bermuda shorts. Before long the shadows fell away to reveal wavy hair, dazzling cheekbones, and a wide smile.

Perhaps it *was* a mirage. After all, a smile from Ryan Taylor was as rare as a diamond in a bag of charcoal. But when he swept her up in his strong arms and held her close, pressing her urgently against his chest, she felt the beat of his heart come in time with her own.

No, she wasn't imagining things at all. She was back in Ryan Taylor's arms.

"No men, no way, nohow," Nina said out loud as she stretched out on her bed. Sliding her arms behind her head, she gazed at the ceiling and said even louder, "And that's final!"

"Talking to yourself?" A voice startled her.

Nina bolted up. Jessica was standing in the doorway, a mischievous smile on her face and two diet sodas in her hands. *I knew I should have locked that door,* Nina thought ungraciously.

Uninvited, Jessica marched in and handed her a can before plopping down on the edge of the bed. "I was getting bored. Liz is off somewhere swooning over Ryan and . . ." She hesitated and stared down at her diet Coke.

Ah, now we're getting to the truth, Nina thought. "And Ben is where?" she asked, brushing back her hair.

Jessica shrugged and ran a finger around the rim of her can. "He's here, and he's sleeping, so I thought you might like some company."

"If you're here to nag me about guys, Jessica, forget it." Nina squared her jaw. "I'm taking a sabbatical." She took a long drink of soda and coughed, choking a little on the bubbles.

Jessica patted her on the back. "I believe you, Nina, really," she said soothingly, a grin spreading across her face. "At least for now."

Jessica just doesn't get it, Nina fumed silently. *Does she think* everyone *is as man-crazy as she is?*

"So . . . ," Jessica began, "do you think there'll be any hot new guys on the squad this summer?"

Nina exhaled loudly. "I don't know and I don't care. I hate to be rude, Jessica, but I still have to unpack." Nina glanced significantly at her two bags.

Jessica rose to her feet. "I get the hint," she said loftily, sailing out the door. "I'm not stupid."

"No, you're just nosy," Nina said softly to herself. She set down her diet Coke and opened one of her bags. On top of the pile of clothing was a sleek, melon-colored one-piece, cut high on the legs. It was one of her sexier bathing suits. Whenever Paul had seen her in it, his eyes had practically fallen out of his head.

Paul Jackson sure kept me in a tailspin last summer, Nina mused as she crumpled the suit up in a ball and stashed it in her bottom dresser drawer. *No way am I letting that happen to me this time around.*

"Oh, Ryan." Elizabeth drank in the fresh, clean scent of Ryan's smooth skin as he held her. Instinctively Elizabeth turned her head to give him a kiss but stopped herself; she couldn't push things too far. She didn't know just how he felt about her—not yet. Elizabeth was relieved in spite of herself when Ryan gently set her back down on the ground and stepped back, his hands gentle but firm on her shoulders.

"I can't believe it," Ryan said softly, deeply. His brown eyes searched hers so closely, she could see their gold flecks glinting in the moonlight. "When I saw you just now, I thought I was dreaming."

"Me too."

"I wasn't sure it was you at first."

28

"What if I had turned out to be Jessica?" she teased, struggling to keep her voice casual as she fell in step beside him. "She would have thought you'd lost your mind."

"Lucky guess on my part." Ryan laughed softly. "Just teasing. When did you get here?"

"About an hour ago," Elizabeth answered. "Were we the last ones to arrive?"

Ryan nodded and moved closer to the water, his gaze fixed straight ahead. "The gang's all here now. We've got a decent crew. And we don't have to worry about getting into any scrapes with the South Beach Squad this time around."

"Why?" Elizabeth asked. "Is it because of Rachel Max?"

"Yeah," Ryan replied quietly. "After those stunts Rachel pulled last summer to mess up the merit-pay competition, the competition's been canned for good. The city decided the lifeguards should concentrate on their jobs instead of on sabotaging rival squads."

"Imagine that," Elizabeth joked. "It's too bad, though. The competition did turn out to be fun."

Ryan shrugged. "Lifeguarding isn't about competition or having fun, Elizabeth. Saving lives is the bottom line. Always." His voice was serious, impersonal. Even in the darkness

Elizabeth could tell Ryan's face was clouding over.

Well, one thing sure hasn't changed, she thought miserably. *Ryan's just as moody and inscrutable as ever.* Suddenly she found herself tripping over a sudden dip in the sand. She gasped, and Ryan rushed over, grabbed her elbow, and steadied her before she could fall. "Thanks," she said, her voice trembling.

Ryan released her arm just as quickly as he grabbed it. "It's tricky out here in the dark," he mumbled.

I'll say it's tricky, especially when a person doesn't know where she stands with you, Elizabeth replied silently.

"Now we're getting somewhere," Nina said as she carefully lined up all her lifeguard necessities on top of her dresser: sunscreen, moisturizer, and sunglasses. She turned back to her bags and sighed as she held up a slinky white sleeveless dress.

"Why did I bring this?" she asked herself out loud. "I'm certainly not out to impress anyone!" For a second she was tempted to ball up the dress and throw it in the wastebasket. But common sense came to the rescue. *I'll put it way in the back of the closet, where it will wait till it's time to go home,* she decided firmly.

A vision of Paul Jackson's handsome face and beautiful brown eyes made her breath catch in her throat. She remembered how he looked wearing nothing but swim trunks, his gorgeous, coffee-with-cream skin, and that sexy smile. But suddenly he seemed far, far away and last summer seemed like a very long time ago.

I could always call him, she told herself. *It's not like we lost touch.* They had talked on the phone a few times, and Paul had always sounded happy to hear from her. They'd even exchanged Christmas cards.

"Wait a minute!" Nina smacked her hand against her forehead. "I've *got* to get off the crazy train *now.*" Groaning, Nina pushed her partially full duffel bags against the wall with her foot and crawled back onto her bed to lie down. "Men are trouble. I don't need any trouble. End of story."

The room began to fade around her, and the sound of the surf coming from the open window was soothing. Nina's eyelids grew heavier and heavier.

A fuzzy picture began to form in Nina's sleepy mind. Her alleged dream guy materialized: tall and muscular, with really toned calves and a small tattoo on his bulging bicep. His face seemed a little foggy—the bright sun seemed to be blurring his features—but she was sure he was waiting for her on a deserted island, his arms outstretched. Behind him palm trees waved in the breeze. The water was crystal clear and peaceful. As Nina came closer she noticed the killer smile on his face, beaming more brightly than the sun.

"I've been waiting for you, Nina," he said in a voice that was devastatingly sexy, yet sweet and yearning too. "What took you so long?"

Helplessly, as if drawn against her will, Nina started toward him. But suddenly another girl brushed past her. Mr. Wonderful turned his head as if on cue, his killer smile now leering and lecherous. Were his teeth turning to fangs?

Suddenly Nina found herself floating above the scene, watching herself step even closer to Prince Not-so-charming. She then saw herself carefully take a step back, bend her leg, and firmly plant her knee in his stomach. He buckled over and fell to the ground.

From her skyborne perch Nina smiled and applauded herself before drifting more deeply into a restful, satisfying sleep.

"The surf looks pretty flat," Ryan commented as he waded into the water. His powerful, tanned legs kicked up sand and foam.

As she watched him Elizabeth couldn't suppress the feeling of warmth that was rising up within her like a riptide. But instead of giving in to it, Elizabeth just felt uncomfortable, as if she were getting worked up over a statue.

That's just what Ryan is—a man of stone, she realized. *But he wasn't always like that. What we shared last summer was tender and beautiful. But now he's acting as if I'm not even here. How can he run so hot, then so cold?*

Swallowing her doubts, Elizabeth rolled her chinos up to her knees and joined him. The cool water was refreshing and brought her spirits up a tiny notch.

In the moonlight Ryan even looks *like a statue,* she mused dreamily. *A statue of a Greek god.*

"Should be a pretty calm beginning to the season," Ryan remarked, pausing to stare out at the horizon. "No wild weather or giant waves to worry about."

"That's good," Elizabeth replied absently, her eye caught by a floating piece of driftwood. She picked it up, brushed the sand off it, and clutched it tightly, wishing it was Ryan's hand. *But perhaps his hand would feel the same—like cold, dead wood.* Her heart sank at the thought.

"But as long we have people on the beach, we can count on having problems," Ryan warned. "Too many people lack common sense."

Is he talking about us? Elizabeth wondered, wincing. *He probably thinks it'd be foolish to get*

33

involved again. That's it—it's over. She hurled the driftwood into the sea and watched it disappear.

Ryan touched her arm lightly. "Want to sit by the dunes for a while? It's a perfect night to watch the sea." He turned away before giving her a chance to answer.

"OK," Elizabeth agreed, her arm tingling from where he touched her. She followed him several feet up into the dunes, where he found a smooth slope of packed sand, perfect for resting. As they settled onto the perch Elizabeth wrapped her arms around her knees and rubbed her upper arms. Despite Ryan's closeness, the evening chill was deepening.

"Cold?" Ryan asked, slipping an arm around her waist and pulling her to him.

Immediately all the coldness she was feeling disappeared, and Elizabeth risked snuggling closer to Ryan. He didn't protest. *A good sign,* she thought happily. *Very good.*

"Elizabeth," Ryan whispered. "If you only knew . . ."

"Yes?" Elizabeth inched closer, gazing up at him.

Ryan's golden-brown eyes burned into hers. "Not too long ago, I thought I had my life all figured out." He stopped. "And now—" He gazed off into the horizon again.

"Everything's changed?" Elizabeth breathed, finishing his sentence. "For the better, I hope. I . . . I know it has for me."

"I never thought I would miss someone as much as I missed you, Liz," Ryan said softly. "I know I haven't done a great job of telling you, but . . . well, now you know."

"I understand," Elizabeth answered quaveringly. For a moment Ryan gripped her around the waist so tightly it almost hurt; he let go and gently cupped her face instead. Elizabeth sighed in sweet relief. She felt his breath on her lips as he brought his face closer to hers. The tips of their noses just barely touched.

"Oh, Liz," Ryan murmured. "You're really here."

"Yes, Ryan. I'm here."

Finally Ryan's mouth met hers, first tenderly, than passionately. She was instantly lost, her head swimming and heart thudding against her chest; the world seemed to disappear when Ryan rained silken kisses all over her face. Then Ryan's lips found hers again. He and Elizabeth clung to each other for what seemed an eternity, until finally they broke apart, gasping for air. The only other sound was the roaring of the ocean, the waves crashing in time with their breaths.

After a few seconds—it could have been minutes

or hours—Elizabeth reached up and smoothed back his sun-streaked, wavy hair. "I'm so happy we're back together, Ryan."

"Me too," he replied, his gaze growing distant for just a brief instant. "But sometimes . . ."

"Sometimes what?" Elizabeth asked, her eyebrows raised in alarm. *Please, Ryan,* she pleaded silently. *If something's wrong, just come out and tell me. I can't take much more of this hot-and-cold act.*

"Sometimes . . . ," Ryan repeated softly, tracing her face with one finger. "Sometimes people waste time talking when they could be doing *better* things."

Relief washed over Elizabeth as she saw the corners of Ryan's eyes crinkle mischievously. "You're absolutely right," she agreed, leaning over to gently kiss his cheek. "So what are we waiting for?"

"We're not," Ryan answered her firmly, tilting her chin up with his finger and guiding her lips toward his. "Not anymore."

A sharp tingle plucked Elizabeth's spine as she gave herself fully to Ryan's embrace. *This,* she thought giddily, *is the* perfect *way to start the summer.*

"He's a goner," Jessica gloated as she leafed through a stack of fashion magazines on her bed. "I'm telling you, Izzy. It was amazing. Ben's *totally* in love with me—he practically fell into my arms!"

Isabella Ricci's dulcet voice vibrated over the phone wires. "That's great, Jess. I know you were a little worried—"

"Ha!" Jessica scoffed, pulling her finger free from the cord. "I was never really worried, just excited. So how are things going in New York?"

Isabella cleared her throat. "Well, I guess things are going as well for me as they are for you. Orlina's Boutique is right in the middle of Madison Avenue, Jess, you should see it! And my boss Angelique, the head buyer, is the greatest. She's teaching me a lot about the industry."

Listening to her friend's voice, Jessica could almost picture Isabella's luminous face glowing with excitement. "Do you get to try on tons of gorgeous clothes?"

"That's a big part of it, plus Angelique wants me to check out all the funky downtown boutiques and report on what people our age are wearing and buying," Isabella explained breathlessly. "She might even take me to see the fall collections in Paris! I'm *so* lucky to have gotten this internship."

Jessica felt a twinge of envy. "You *are* lucky, Iz, but so am I. Ben and I are going to have the *whole* summer to really get to know each other."

Jessica lowered her voice. "This is going to be the romance of a lifetime, Iz. I've *never* felt this way before."

After a silence from Isabella, Jessica heaved a big sigh. "I know, I know. I've said this before, but this time it's different." Jessica stretched and flexed her slim legs out in front of her. "Ben isn't like any of the men I've known. He *understands* me."

"I'm not arguing with you, Jess. I just want you to go slowly. Don't forget, it's been a while since you've seen Ben, and people can change."

"Well, Ben and I haven't changed at all," Jessica said, her voice brimming with confidence. "We're solid."

"Congratulations are in order, then," Isabella said. "I suppose you two are celebrating tonight. Don't tell me—you're going out for a midnight picnic on the beach."

"*We*-ell, not exactly." Jessica squirmed a little. Isabella's suggestion sounded so romantic that Jessica was overcome with frustrated longing. "Ben was supertired and went to bed early. I'm tempted to go wake him up." A wicked smile flitted across Jessica's face as she imagined just how she would rouse him from his nap.

"Oooh!"

"But I think I'll wait on that." Jessica sighed in resignation. "A good summer romance, like a fine wine, takes time."

Isabella giggled. "Jessica Wakefield. Always the philosopher."

"Besides, we both have to report to work tomorrow at seven sharp," Jessica chirped. "What good would it do for us to show up all bleary-eyed and rumpled?"

Chapter Three

"Go away, Nina, please!" Elizabeth moaned, her head buried under her pillow. All she wanted to do was drift back to that beautiful dream she'd been having about Ryan. But when Nina continued banging on the door, she wished she could snap her fingers and make her best friend disappear. Elizabeth knew it was Friday morning, the first day on the job and the first day of the big summer opening weekend, but she couldn't rouse herself. She just wasn't ready to leave the peaceful comfort of her bed and the lingering memory of Ryan's arms.

"Elizabeth Wakefield, if you don't open this door right now, I'll come in there and drag you down to the beach in your pajamas!" Nina shouted. "We're going to be late if you don't hop to it."

Slowly, reluctantly Elizabeth sat up. "OK, Nina," she called hoarsely. "I'm coming."

"You'd better be," Nina warned. "Or I'll personally call up Ryan and read him the riot act."

"I'm on my way to the shower now, I promise." Blinking, she waited for Nina's footsteps to retreat. Then she foggily got out from under the covers and put on her slippers.

On any other morning Elizabeth would have sprung out of bed at the crack of dawn, full of energy. But since she'd spent half the night reuniting with Ryan, she now felt as if she needed a full twenty-four hours of shut-eye to recover.

In the bathroom she paused and made a face at her sleepy-eyed, tousled-haired reflection in the mirror above the sink. *Serves you right,* she tried to lecture herself, but she couldn't stop a giddy smile from spreading across her face. Ryan was worth the missed sleep. Definitely.

Knowing Ryan, he's probably wide awake and raring to go, she thought affectionately as she jumped into the shower and stood under the sharp needles of hot water.

Twenty minutes later Elizabeth was dressed for work and feeling refreshed as she made her way downstairs. A babble of voices drifted from the kitchen, along with a tantalizing scent. Elizabeth beamed as she pulled her hair up into a neat ponytail. Blueberry pancakes—she'd recognize that yummy aroma anywhere. And she instantly knew who the cook was too.

"I don't know about anyone else, but I'm starving," Elizabeth said, floating into the kitchen and slipping into the nearest empty chair.

Nina, Jessica, and Ben were all seated around the table, nodding. They looked wide awake and sharp. Like Elizabeth, Nina and Jessica were dressed in matching red tank suits and crisp white nylon jackets with Sweet Valley Shore Lifeguard Squad silk-screened over their hearts. Ben's red trunks were capped with a white tank top; he wore his jacket tied around his waist.

"I think we're all in agreement here," Nina quipped as she adjusted the Velcro strap on one of her waterproof athletic shoes. "If we don't eat soon, someone will have to save *our* lives."

A tall, skinny man in a Kiss the Cook apron and a white peaked chef's cap turned from the stove. "At your service, milady," Winston Egbert said dramatically. "Your wish is my command. Breakfast is ready." He bowed deeply and gestured to the griddle full of perfect, golden cakes. When he straightened up, Winston's cap dropped down over his eyes and he blindly jerked upright, knocking his head into the open cabinet door above the stove.

"Oops and ouch." Winston groaned. His glasses suddenly slid down his nose, and the

42

spatula he waved wildly in his hand hooked into a hanging plant, sending it spinning. A few leaves and dirt floated to the red-and-black parquet floor.

"Same old Winnie." Elizabeth giggled. "A great pancake maker and a one-man floor show! I hope none of the leaves landed in the rest of the batter."

"Not yet," Nina commented dryly, stirring her cup of coffee. "Just give him time."

"I'm being slandered," Winston moped as he flipped golden brown pancakes onto a serving platter. "A master chef never adds foreign objects to his masterpieces."

"At least not intentionally." Ben chuckled. "Well, a little dirt never killed anyone."

"That's right, Winnie," Elizabeth offered. "I'd eat your pancakes in any condition."

"I'm surprised you're hungry at all, Liz," Jessica said slyly. "You look like the cat that ate the canary. If you grin any harder, your face will break."

Elizabeth blushed. Did everyone know she'd been out with Ryan last night?

"Now, now, Jess," Ben joked. "People will think you're jealous."

Jessica made a face. "Like *I've* ever cared what other people think."

"Like you've ever cared that people actually *do* think."

"Cheap shot number two," Jessica drawled. "Three strikes, you're out."

When Elizabeth took a good look at her twin, she was stunned. Jessica's hair, which she usually wore loose, was sleek and glistening in a French braid with a red ribbon woven through it. A simple ponytail would have been appropriate enough for lifeguarding, but obviously it just wouldn't have been glamorous enough for Jessica today. Her rose-tinted lip gloss matched the polish on the tips of her fingers. Elizabeth sneaked a look down at the floor and saw that Jessica's flawlessly coordinated toenails were peeking out from the open toes of her white leather slip-ons. To top it all off, she was wearing what smelled like her most expensive perfume.

She can't be doing this just for Ben's benefit, can she? Elizabeth wondered. *I didn't think he was the kind of guy who cared about that sort of thing.*

"Everyone!" Winston announced, jolting Elizabeth from her thoughts. "Prepare your palates for the experience of a lifetime." With a flourish he set a platter stacked with blueberry pancakes in the middle of the table next to a dish of butter and a big pitcher of syrup. Everyone grabbed their forks and dove in.

"These are totally scrumptious, Winston,"

Elizabeth said, prompting a chorus of agreement from the rest of the table. "We're really going to miss having you around this summer—and not just for your culinary talents."

Winston turned back to the stove and began pouring more batter onto the crackling pan. "Wendy made me an offer I couldn't refuse," Winston explained. "When she invited me to stay at the Paloma beach house for the summer, how could I say no? Wendy really needed the company since Pedro's on tour again."

"How is Wendy doing?" Elizabeth broke in impatiently. "I already miss her too."

"She's doing great," Winston replied. "Better than ever."

Tall, thin Wendy Wolman had been another one of their housemates the previous summer. Her plain appearance belied her sharp sense of humor and bubbly personality. After a strange series of coincidences Winston had managed to set her up on a date with her idol, Pedro Paloma, the famous, handsome singer. By the end of the summer they had gotten engaged, and now Wendy Wolman had become Wendy Paloma.

Thanks to the song he'd written about her, "The Girl with Smoke-Colored Eyes," Pedro had become a household name and was selling out stadiums all over the world. Elizabeth had even seen an hour-long special about him on one of the music channels.

"How's their new beach house?" Nina asked.

"You mean beach *mansion*," Winston corrected. "When a place is that huge and expensive, it's no longer a house. The place is a little intimidating, but I think I'll get used to it."

Elizabeth laughed. "It's hard to believe that someone so unconcerned with material things would end up getting married to a wealthy superstar and living in a huge mansion."

"It's not hard to believe at all," Winston said proudly. "Wendy and Pedro are a match made in heaven. And don't forget, *I'm* the one who made it."

"Don't worry, we haven't forgotten." Jessica groaned. "It's too bad we missed their wedding, though. I bet there were lots of celebrities there."

"There were. I've seen the pictures," Winston said loftily.

"Like who?" Jessica breathed, eyes wide.

"That's for me to know and you to find out. You should stop by sometime and check out Wendy's wedding album." Winston added more pancakes to the serving platter and sat down. "Speaking of secrecy, I've got a big interview lined up this afternoon."

"What kind of job is it?" Nina asked, folding

her napkin. "Not lifeguarding, I'm sure."

Everyone laughed. Elizabeth remembered how miserably Winston had failed the lifeguard trials last summer. He'd ended up having to parade around in a gigantic hamburger costume to drum up business for Hamburger Harry's food stand. Not only that, but Winston had taken his job a step further by staging fights with rival food-stand mascot Hot Dog Howie.

"Sorry, but my lips are sealed." Winston smiled and made a motion of zipping his mouth.

"C'mon, you can tell us," Jessica urged.

Winston merely shook his head and ate the last bite of his pancake.

"I know!" Elizabeth snapped her fingers, her eyes gleaming. "You're going to be Pedro's promoter. After your success as a human hamburger, Pedro'd be crazy not put your flair for showmanship to good use."

Winston chuckled. "All I can say is that I've come upon a rare opportunity and—"

"Did you say *rare?*" Jessica interrupted, giggling. "Gee, Hamburger Harry, we always thought you were *well-done.*"

"But hey, that's not to say we don't *relish* you, man," Ben chimed in, his blue eyes sparkling with mischief.

Nina leaned forward and tapped Winston

with her fork. "Even though we're no longer waiting for you to *ketchup* with us in the water," she added, grinning broadly.

Ignoring Winston's loud groans, Elizabeth concluded, "Don't feel bad, Winston. As a friend and a pancake chef, you really cut the *mustard!*"

"Ha, ha." Winston got up from the table and started collecting dirty dishes. "You guys kill me, you really do." His eyes were twinkling behind his glasses, though his face was contorted into an expression of mock outrage. "Elizabeth, I'm crushed. I never guessed *you'd* join in the pun assault."

Elizabeth cut a neat triangle into a pancake, her dimple flashing in her left cheek. "Just be glad we didn't start talking about your sesame-covered *buns!*"

C'mon, Ben, Jessica commanded silently as she and Ben headed across the beach toward the lifeguard station. *I know you're crazy about me, so why don't you just admit it?*

She fidgeted with her uncomfortable French braid, wincing as it pinched her temples. *You haven't even kissed me yet. What are you waiting for?*

"Um, I'm glad we're starting work today," Jessica said casually. It was a gorgeous morning;

48

the beach looked picture-perfect, with gentle azure waves rolling up against it and the glistening sun rising across a flawless blue sky. "I'm totally ready. I hope I get a post with a lot of action."

"Don't count on it," Ben said, chuckling. "You know Ryan. He sticks to his own agenda." The sun highlighted every hard ridge and ripple on his forearms and legs. He looked so cute in his red regulation trunks that it was hard for Jessica not to throw her arms around him.

"At least I know I'm in good shape," Jessica said, fishing for compliments. She slipped off her nylon jacket and fastened it around her slender waist, just like Ben had. They'd almost reached the station, and she was hoping Ben would hurry up and say something romantic while they were still alone. "You know, I've been exercising like crazy."

"You look good," Ben said hastily, "so don't worry about it."

"Thanks. I won't," she answered demurely. As they got closer she spotted two strange figures. But everything else looked just the same; it was her Sweet Valley Shore. Jessica smiled, recognizing the long, wooden, one-storied station with its red flag flying from the roof. She turned to drink in the familiar breathtaking coastal view of the beach.

"Hey, Ben, my man! It's about time," a deep voice called, startling Jessica from her reverie. A tall, lean African American man was beckoning to Ben, a welcoming smile on his model-handsome face. He and a pretty girl Jessica had never seen before were standing a few yards away. The guy had an incredible physique, lean and muscled.

What a babe, Jessica thought almost reflexively.

"Hey, Theo!" Ben shouted back, grinning widely. "'Scuse me, Jess," he said before trotting off toward his friend with barely a backward glance.

Jessica scowled. *That must be the buddy he helped get onto the squad,* she thought, watching jealously as Ben slapped the new guy on the back. *This Theo guy must know all about Ben and me. So why doesn't Ben introduce us?* To conceal her annoyance, Jessica adjusted the strap of her suit and forced a smile on her face. She wouldn't let Ben see her sulking.

The new girl walked over to introduce herself. "Hi, I'm Miranda Reese," she said with a warm smile, her wide brown eyes sparkling. She reached out her hand. "And you are . . . ?"

"Jessica Wakefield," she replied, shaking her hand. Miranda was a trim and toned Amazon; her shiny brown hair was fastened in a ponytail that brushed her shoulders. She was very pretty, fair skinned with freckles on her small, upturned nose. She was just beginning to show the signs of a light tan. The red lifeguard tank complimented her sculpted, athletic figure.

Miranda jerked her head toward Ben, curiosity gleaming in her eyes. "So how do you know Ben? Did you guys work together last summer?"

Feeling a competitive twinge, Jessica released Miranda's hand. "Mm-hmm. Ben's my boyfriend," she said coolly. "So hands off."

"Oh, I'm not interested in him," Miranda assured her, her eyes widening a little. "I already have a boyfriend back at school. So, you and Ben are really a couple?"

"You bet." Jessica raised her chin and crossed her arms in front of her.

Miranda looked impressed. "That's . . . that's really something. You guys must be sharing the Krebbs place, right? I saw you coming from the same direction."

Jessica nodded. "There're four of us: me, my twin sister, Nina Harper, and Ben. There were six last year, but we had a couple of dropouts."

"That sounds like a great setup," Miranda murmured. "Theo"— she pointed out Ben's gorgeous friend—"and I are sharing a condo. We get along great, but . . ."

"What?" Jessica prompted.

"We've got this major pest problem in the house."

"Ugh! What is it—mice?" Jessica crinkled up her nose.

"No." Miranda grinned slowly. "Priya."

"What?"

Miranda giggled. "Priya Rahman is our housemate and a first-class royal pain in the . . . neck," she explained. "She's a total brat—probably the most conceited person in the world. When Priya's not busy bragging about how intellectual and superior she is, all she does is yap on and on about her precious boyfriend." Miranda shot Jessica a cautioning glance and sighed.

"Don't worry." Jessica tossed her head. "I'm not like that. *I'm* not the type to brag about dating the best-looking guy on Sweet Valley Shore," she said archly with a wink.

Miranda's eyes glinted conspiratorially. "I have a feeling that once you and Priya have met, she'll realize she's met her match." She leaned forward and whispered, "But hopefully you won't have to."

"Why?"

"Poor, pampered little Priya was too tired to get out of bed this morning. 'I'm *so* burnt out from finals and those tryouts were *so* gruesome,'" Miranda mimicked in a falsetto.

"So I just left her there! Maybe she won't show and will get bumped from the squad. I hope so. We'll all be better off."

"I totally agree," Jessica said breezily, watching Ryan as he strode across the dunes toward them, Elizabeth and Nina at his side.

"I bet you do."

Jessica nodded wisely. She and Miranda were obviously on the same wavelength. "We had to deal with someone like Priya last year," she said quickly. "A real snot named Rachel Max, who also happened to be Ben's ex. They even went to the University of Chicago together." Jessica grimaced, remembering how nasty and jealous Rachel had been. "Luckily Rachel won't be back this year. She pulled a major stunt at the merit-pay competition last summer and ended up in handcuffs. It's because of her that the competition has been dropped."

Miranda wrinkled her lightly freckled nose. "I heard about that. She sounds like a total pain."

"She was, but Ben made it clear who he wanted to be with," Jessica assured her. She glanced over at Ben, who was laughing at something Theo was saying. His handsome grin sent a surge of pride through Jessica's chest.

Miranda didn't respond. She stopped and walked a few feet away to dig out sunscreen from a small orange tote in the sand. Busily she applied some lotion to her shoulders.

Jessica nodded approvingly. "Good idea, Miranda. You want to get tanned, not crisped. So what about you? You don't happen to go to the U of C, do you?"

Miranda shook her head. "Nope, Bard."

"Sweet Valley University," Jessica answered. "Speaking of Sweet Valley, how do you like it here?"

Miranda tucked the sunscreen back into her tote. "It's not too bad," she said, standing up. "It reminds me of my campus. Kind of small, but loaded with babes."

Jessica and Miranda shared a giggle.

"Attention, everyone, let's get started," Ryan interrupted, frowning into the sun. He looked down at his clipboard and then up, scanning everyone's faces. "Some of us are old-timers and some of us are new here." Ryan began gesturing to the members of his team circled around him. "Elizabeth Wakefield, Jessica Wakefield, and Nina Harper, meet Miranda Reese, Theo Moore, and Priya Rahman. You all know Ben Mercer already." Ryan suddenly looked around, scowling. "Wait, where is Priya anyway? Does anyone know?"

Jessica caught Miranda's eye and smirked. "Does anyone *care?*"

"Uh, Ryan, I'm sure Priya's on her way,"

Ben offered, his face reddening. "She's probably running a little late . . . as usual."

As usual? Jessica felt an icy finger of unease crawl up her spine. *How would Ben know?*

Ryan's scowl deepened. "'A little late' and 'late' are the same thing, Ben. We can't wait for her. If she's not here in—"

"Sorry!"

Jessica whirled around to see a petite woman racing across the sand toward them, waving her arms. She was wearing a red lifeguard tank suit, but in place of the regulation white jacket was a lace cover-up. It contrasted sharply with her deep bronze skin and long, thick, gleaming black hair.

That must be Priya—and she's drop-dead gorgeous! Jessica realized as the woman drew closer. *Miranda never mentioned* that.

"There you are, sweetie!"

"What?" Jessica whirled around to see Ben waving at the latecomer, his smile wide and expectant.

Jessica smirked. *He's just trying to make me jealous. I know it.*

But the sight of Ben Mercer opening his arms and sweeping the latecomer into a hug made her stomach do a triple somersault and her blood congeal in her veins. Her hands curled into fists. Her chest felt as tight as if she were wearing a corset three sizes too small.

"It's about time, Priya," Ben scolded affectionately. "You kept everyone waiting. But you're worth every minute." His tone was so sweet, it could have been poured over ice cream and topped with a cherry.

"I know," Priya purred before Ben leaned down and gave her a long, lingering, and utterly romantic kiss.

Jessica opened her mouth to say something, but words escaped her. She could only stand there, immobile, with hot tears burning behind her eyes as she watched the truth unfold and her world fall apart.

"I'm sorry, Jessica," Nina whispered under her breath. "I tried to warn you." Even though Jessica's constant stream of boy-crazy chatter had driven her up a tree, Nina couldn't help but sympathize when she saw the effect Ben's little performance had on her. She looked as if she had been stabbed through the heart. Which, in Nina's mind, was exactly what had just happened.

I can't say I'm surprised, Nina realized. *After all, Ben and Bryan were buddies in high school. It must have been something in the cafeteria food.* She exhaled sharply. *No—the Υ chromosome is to blame, plain and simple.*

A sudden, nauseating vision of Bryan with the faceless, syrupy-voiced, phone-answering female made a sharp throbbing begin behind Nina's eyes.

Did *she* look like Priya too?

Nina could just see Bryan with his hands all over the other woman, murmuring sweet lies and not giving Nina a second thought. Gritting her teeth, she dug her nails into her palm. *All men are disgusting, and that's a fact.*

"Did you say something, Nina?" Ryan asked, glancing up from his clipboard.

"No," she muttered, catching Elizabeth's eye. Her best friend was standing behind Ryan, mindlessly twirling the end of her ponytail and trying to smile. Her face was white and strained. *She's trying to keep cool for Jessica's sake*, Nina guessed. She knew both sisters were proud and fiercely loyal. She also knew they could be tigers when protecting each other. But this was a bad time to make a scene.

The throbbing behind Nina's eyes began mercilessly spreading across her entire head. *Me and Bryan. Jessica and Ben. It's all the same.*

"Are you all right, Nina?" Ryan took off his sunglasses and stared at her. "You look a little under the weather."

"I am," Nina admitted, swallowing hard. The pain was bad, but not bad enough to keep her from realizing that she was now feeling queasy too. "I have an incredible headache. Do you have any aspirin?"

"You look like you need more than aspirin, Nina," Elizabeth said anxiously.

"She's right. You do look pretty shaky," Ryan agreed. "Since it looks like a slow day, take the day off and rest up for tomorrow."

"OK."

Elizabeth came over and touched her arm softly. "Do you want me to walk back with you?"

Nina shook her head and thanked her. She knew Jessica needed all the help she could get. *All I need is some peace and quiet,* Nina thought as she headed to the beach house. The pain in her head throbbed with each step. *Maybe a nunnery would do.*

A few yards ahead a thin, long-haired man in raggedy jeans was setting up a small tent and jabbing a sign into the sand. A tower of large, brightly colored inner tubes was stacked beside the tent.

The sight of inner tubes sent Nina flying back in time, back to when happiness came easily, when an ice cream bar and a sand castle were all she needed. Nina's father always brought a big inner tube for Nina to play with in the water, whether they were at her grandparents' lake house or at the ocean. Nina remembered how soothing it had been to stretch across the inner tube, her legs and arms draping over the sides and trailing into the water. She'd let waves carry her off as the sun warmed her face. Her parents would call to her and wave, big, proud smiles on their faces.

Those were the days, Nina thought dreamily. *Life was so easy back then.* If she could get in touch with those feelings again, it would be the perfect remedy.

Nina walked over to the inner tube man. "How much?" she asked quickly.

"Usually twenty dollars an hour," the man replied, slapping a sombrero onto his head and settling into a lawn chair. He looked her up and down with a little grin. "But for you, cutie—fifteen dollars."

Nina rolled her eyes. "No, *twenty,* I insist," she growled as she unzipped the waterproof pocket in her nylon jacket and handed him the money. Purposefully she strode over and grabbed the cheerful-looking lemon yellow inner tube on top of the stack.

She rolled the inner tube to the water's edge, feeling more and more relaxed as she went along. Despite the insistent breeze the ocean was calm and as blue as the Wakefield twins' eyes. A few sandpipers skittered out of Nina's way as she waded into waist-high water. Then she climbed aboard, not even bothering to take off her light jacket.

Ahhh, yes, she thought happily as she settled onto the inner tube. *This is what I need. Peace, quiet, and a total escape from the male species.*

The water was pungent and a little cold, but the sun felt deliciously warm in comparison. The waves moved the tube out into deeper and deeper water. Drowsily Nina pulled some strands of seaweed that had wrapped around her leg and tossed them aside.

Perfect, Nina thought as she drifted away from shore. The sun's rays felt like gentle, warm fingers caressing her face. Nina crossed her hands behind her head and smiled. Now she was perfectly relaxed, her body in the most comfortable position. The slop-whoosh of the waves was like a lullaby. A soothing, hypnotic lullaby. Her breathing slowed, and her body grew limp. Every muscle in her body felt like wet tissue paper.

Nina's lids grew heavier and heavier. The shimmering water and bright sunlight melted together into a lovely haze. The world began to recede. The last thing Nina heard was a distant cry of a seagull before she sank into the velvety abyss of sleep.

Chapter Four

I can't believe it! Jessica shook with rage as she watched Ben and Priya head off toward Tower 3. *Nina was right. Men really are dogs!*

"Maybe I should strangle Ben with my whistle strap," Jessica muttered as she toyed with the lifeguard's whistle hanging around her neck. *Naturally Ryan paired Ben and Velcro Girl together,* she thought feverishly. *He must have realized that she couldn't even walk without clinging on to Ben's arm.*

Jessica groaned when she saw Ben suddenly tickle Priya, who giggled in an affected tone so high, it made Jessica's teeth ache. For some reason Priya seemed to get prettier every minute, with her smooth, caramel-flan skin, her long, thick hair that Jessica could have sworn was a wig, and a body that rivaled Barbie's.

Suddenly Jessica put her hand to her chest. Maybe she was hyperventilating. Maybe she would even pass out. Now *that* would get everyone's attention . . .

. . . everyone's but Ben's. Since Priya came on the scene, he never once glanced Jessica's way.

When Ben scooped up his beautiful girlfriend and threw her over his shoulder, Jessica held back the urge to retch. Throwing up on the beach would attract a little *too* much attention. *They're so disgustingly cute, like they're straight out of a soda commercial,* she thought, absently becoming aware that someone was talking to her and tapping on her arm—hard.

"Jessica," Miranda said with a big, phony grin. "I said, isn't it great that we have Tower Two? I saw a ton of cute guys playing Frisbee down there." Miranda's voice sounded foghorn loud in Jessica's ringing ears.

Jessica tried to ignore her new partner. *What is her problem? Can't she see how I feel?* she wondered. *If she wants to be my friend so bad, why couldn't she have warned me about this?*

But after a minute or two everything began to sink in. If Miranda *had* gone ahead and told Jessica the truth, she never would have believed it anyway. Besides, maybe Miranda was actually hoping that Jessica was Ben's *real* girlfriend and that Priya would end up getting dumped like last week's garbage. *I guess she was only trying to protect me,* she told herself. *And now she's only trying to cheer me up.*

Still, it was hardly any consolation that she had been crushed, dissected, and mutilated by Ben in front of everyone and the only person coming to her aid was practically a total stranger. Jessica tried to stop the tears from welling up again by watching a family of five beachgoers who had emerged from over the horizon. The parents were loaded down with chairs, a picnic basket, beach toys, and an umbrella while their three small children raced around in circles and squealed at the top of their lungs.

"Look, Jessica, I'm sorry I didn't tell you before, but it seemed like the wrong thing to do after I just met you," Miranda offered. "Try and pull yourself together. You don't want to give Ben the satisfaction of seeing you fall apart, do you?"

"Maybe I do," Jessica said hotly. "Maybe I do."

"Here." Elizabeth handed Ryan his binoculars. She'd just come from the tower supply room. Standing behind his chair on the main tower, she paused to take a deep breath of fresh sea air. The sun was rising higher and getting hotter by the minute, but a soft, cool breeze was coming in from the bay. Elizabeth reached around to kiss his cheek. *He smells so good, like coconut and the ocean.* As her lips brushed his smooth, deeply browned skin she couldn't help thinking, *And he tastes good too.*

"Hey," Ryan said with mock sternness as he pushed his sunglasses back up his nose. "No mixing business with pleasure." He pulled her to him for a quick kiss. When they broke away, he was quickly distracted by something on the beach. He grabbed his binoculars and peered through them, frowning.

"What's wrong?" Elizabeth asked, squinting out at the surf.

"It's that family," he answered, pointing to three young, fair-haired children and their weary-looking parents. "They're an accident waiting to happen." Ryan sighed and scratched his jaw. "Both adults are falling asleep, leaving the kids unsupervised. None of them look like strong swimmers."

Elizabeth nodded understandingly. Despite Ryan's past battle with alcoholism, or maybe because of it, he was a lot more mature and responsible than most guys his age. She knew that Ryan had faced a tragedy a couple of summers ago when a hangover had kept him from work and a child drowned while someone else was on his shift.

Which is why he's supervigilant, Elizabeth thought admiringly as she pulled her sun visor down. A tender smile curved her lips. *But Ryan's more than just a terrific lifeguard—he's an all-around good guy, unlike Ben Mercer.*

Elizabeth automatically scanned the beach and did a head count, but she couldn't get her sister out of her mind. *Poor Jessica was so devastated,* she remembered with increasing anger. *He was really rubbing her nose in it.* The image of her standing there, helpless, totally embarrassed while Ben fawned all over that new girl made Elizabeth's throat close in sympathy. *How dare he treat my sister like that!* Seething, Elizabeth dug her fingers into the tower rail.

"Hey, watch it," Ryan teased. "You don't want to break it, do you? The chair, that is—not Ben Mercer's skull."

Elizabeth turned quickly to face him. "Of course not; it's just that—"

"—you're upset about Jessica?" Ryan finished softly for her. He raked his fingers through his sun-streaked hair. "Try not to worry about your sister, OK? She's tougher than she looks. You know that better than anyone. She and Ben will work it out."

Elizabeth nodded and tried to hide her disappointment. *No one understands how it is to be a twin,* she thought. *When one suffers, the other does too.* "Too bad you had to put Ben and Priya together at the same post," she finally said.

Ryan shrugged. "Ben asked me to as a favor. He was worried Priya might feel uncomfortable with someone she didn't know—"

"Oh, right," Elizabeth retorted sarcastically. "I figured that you, of all people, would know better than to pair up a guy with his girlfriend."

Ryan shook his head and shot her one of his rare smiles, immediately defusing her anger. "Well, if I did that, then I couldn't exactly justify pairing *us*, could I?"

Elizabeth reddened. "I guess you're right," she admitted. "Still, I don't think it's a good idea—"

Ryan suddenly blew his whistle and grabbed his bullhorn. "Hey, stay out of the water!" he bellowed at one of the young children he had been watching earlier. The little boy was toddling toward the nonswimming zone. In response the boy began to cry just as his mother raced over and scooped him up into her arms.

Exhaling sharply, Ryan fell back into his chair. "Well, that's a relief—for now. Some people never learn, though. They can be so predictable." He took off his sunglasses and rubbed his eyes before putting them back on. His face was grim.

"But *sometimes* people can surprise you." Elizabeth leaned over and gave him a quick kiss on the cheek.

Ryan's expression thawed a little. "As a matter of fact, I've been finding that out lately myself." He reached over and lightly smoothed a stray wisp of hair back from her face, then turned back to face the water.

Elizabeth's heart began to pound more insistently. She longed to look deeply into his eyes and see what he was really feeling, but he had his sunglasses on; they were the perfect mask.

"You know, Ben and I were really close, um, last summer," Jessica complained from Tower 2. "I can't believe he'd treat me like—like yesterday's news!"

"Me either," Miranda agreed as she smoothed on more sunscreen.

"I just don't get it. I must be crazy or something. I mean, how can he hang out with that fakey little witch?"

"I honestly don't know," Miranda responded soothingly. "Think about it this way, Jessica—what happened *after* last summer? Did you stay tight? Write letters and call each other every weekend?"

Jessica stared at her rosy-tipped big toe and avoided Miranda's gaze. "Uh, that's kind of the problem," she admitted. "Ben and I lost touch after a while, and it was kind of my fault. I just stopped writing back and calling. I don't know why!" Her voice ended on a wail.

Miranda nodded. "These things happen."

"It's just that long-distance relationships are so *hard*. I couldn't handle it."

Miranda slid on her wraparound, green-rimmed sunglasses. "So he thinks you blew him off, and maybe now he's getting back at you," she said thoughtfully. "Did he even mention Priya to you after you got here?"

"No!" Jessica burst out angrily. "He deliberately lied to me. He never told me the *friend* he was helping through tryouts was a *girl!*" Jessica squinted into the sun. She needed her sunglasses but had left them back in the beach house.

"I'm sorry, Jessica, really." Miranda opened her tote and handed Jessica an extra pair of sunglasses. "I really should have said something when we were talking before. But I honestly didn't know what to think when you said Ben was your boyfriend, so I kept my mouth shut."

"It's not your fault, Miranda. He was flirting with me and everything. He led me on," Jessica said furiously. "He acted like nothing had changed."

"Hmmm. Looks like you've got a boyfriend out for revenge."

"*Ex*-boyfriend." Jessica spat out each syllable. "But if he thinks I'm going to disappear gracefully and take this like a good sport, he's got another thing coming." With a derisive glance toward Tower 3, Jessica untied the jacket from her waist and tossed it onto the platform. Then she began shinnying down the ladder to the beach.

"Go get him," Miranda urged with a big grin. "Show no mercy!"

"Don't worry, I won't," Jessica hissed.

"Take no prisoners!"

"Ha! They'll need body bags when I get finished with them." Jessica jumped down onto the sand. She took a deep breath and exhaled sharply.

Miranda saluted and snapped to attention. "Private, you have your orders. Report back to me when it's over."

"You'll get full details. I promise." Jessica spun around and faced Tower 3. "This mission will be a success."

Miranda giggled wickedly. "Maybe you'll scare her so bad, she'll go back home. We can always hope." She paused for a moment to adjust her sunglasses. "No matter what happens, let's go out tonight and have some fun. We'll form the She-Woman-Ben-Hater's Club!"

Jessica laughed. "Sounds great. Now, if you'll excuse me, there are a couple of rats I need to exterminate. *I'll be back*," she joked in her best Arnold Schwarzenegger voice.

As she made her way to Tower 3 Jessica

murmured, "Sorry, Ben, but you know the rules. No dogs allowed on the beach."

At the main tower Elizabeth tried desperately to hold down her anxiety. For nearly five minutes Ryan had been absolutely silent. Every time she would clear her throat to speak, he remained stone-faced and inaccessible. She couldn't hold out any longer.

"You know, Ryan, I have a good feeling about this summer," she offered, taking the plunge. "Don't you?"

Ryan didn't answer for a few seconds. Finally he said softly, "I hope so, Liz."

"C'mon," she teased. "You can do better than that."

Ryan just shrugged.

Now what's wrong? Elizabeth wondered, frustrated. She knew that sometimes being patient and waiting out Ryan's spells was the only thing to do, so she focused her attention on the surf. *I am here to work, after all,* she reminded herself. The ocean waves were quick and steady, but not dangerously rough. Maybe the rest of the morning would be uneventful.

"Liz."

Ryan's voice startled her. She turned to face him.

He touched her shoulder. "Thanks for hanging

in there," he said softly. "I—I'm sorry if I've been spacing out on you. But I've just had a lot on my mind lately."

Elizabeth's heart sank. "Like what?" she asked cautiously.

Ryan shook his head. "Don't worry. It has nothing to do with you and me," he said, taking her hand and kissing it.

Despite her curiosity, Elizabeth felt a happy smile spread across her face. "So you're saying that I *haven't* been on your mind?" she joked.

"You're always on my mind." Ryan chuckled. "Listen, I have an idea. If you're not busy tonight, how about getting together for a nice, home-cooked dinner?"

"I'd love to," she answered. "Where, here? At your room in the tower?"

"No, at Patti's apartment."

"That sounds great! I can't wait to see Patti." Elizabeth vividly remembered the day she met Patti Yager, Ryan's A.A. sponsor, after secretly following him to the church where his meetings were held. Ryan hadn't told Elizabeth about his problem yet; at one point she'd actually suspected that Ryan and Patti were getting married! When she saw Ryan stand up in front of his group and talk about his fight to stay sober, her unease over invading his privacy was overcome by her pride and admiration. In the

71

end it brought them even closer together.

"I told Patti you were coming back to the beach, so she suggested we all get together," Ryan mentioned. "Arthur, her husband, will be there too. Does that sound OK?"

"It sounds more than OK."

"Good." Ryan paused for a moment, his features darkening. "This really means a lot to me, Liz."

Elizabeth smiled softly. Even though Ryan had been sober for a long time now, she was fully aware that every day was still a battle for him. "I know," she reassured him, placing her hand over his.

Jessica plastered a smile on her face and took a deep, shaky breath. So far, Ben and Priya were too absorbed in misting each other with water to acknowledge her presence, even though she stood just a few feet away under Tower 3. *They're just pretending they don't see me*, Jessica thought, gritting her teeth. *Either that, or they're obviously too engrossed in each other to recognize trouble if it were on the water . . . or standing right underneath their noses.*

"All this water is making me thirsty." Priya pouted. "I could really use one of your famous milk shakes, Ben. Why don't you make me one later at *my* place?"

Ben grinned. "Sounds good to me," he said eagerly.

Priya giggled coyly. "It's a date, then."

Enough, Jessica told herself. She was uncomfortably conscious of the sun beating down on her scalp while she stood there, ignored and humiliated. *That's it. I've had enough.*

"What's wrong, Ben?" Jessica called out in a dangerously sweet voice. "Do you need cooling off?"

Ben slowly turned and stared down at Jessica for a long, tense second. "I guess I do," he said, smirking. His grin broadened as he draped a muscular arm around Priya's smooth shoulders. "You could say I'm getting a little overheated."

Priya tossed back her sleek hair petulantly. "Are you lost or something, Jennifer? This isn't Tower Two." A mean smile curved Priya's lips. "Maybe Ryan should draw you a map or something."

Jessica felt hot anger bubble up inside her. She brushed a strand of loose hair from her face and planted her feet firmly in the sand. "My name is Jessica—*J-e-s-s-i-c-a.* I guess Ben must have forgotten his manners—he hasn't properly introduced us."

Ben's brilliant blue eyes raked over Jessica's face. "Oh, pardon me," he said airily. "Jessica Wakefield, this is Priya Rahman. I told you about her last night."

73

"Oh, was that *you* I was talking to?" Jessica asked, mimicking Ben's airy tone. "Silly me. I certainly don't remember hearing any mention of a *girl*friend."

Priya's eyes narrowed, then her fakey smile turned vicious. "You really are confused, aren't you? *First* you get lost and forget where your post is, and now this! How on earth do you make it through college?" Her brown eyes sparkled with malice. "Wait, let me guess . . . you're still in high school!"

"For your information, I attend Sweet Valley University," Jessica rasped, grinding her teeth.

Priya stifled a yawn. "Oh yes, Ben mentioned it. SVU is some little local college, right?" Before Jessica could make an angry retort, Priya slid her arm around Ben's waist and continued. "Ben and I are just two of the privileged few who attend the University of Chicago. Our college has a very demanding academic program and very *high* standards."

"They must be slipping if they let you two in."

"There are so few true intellectuals around these days," Ben complained as if he hadn't heard Jessica's comment. "It's almost impossible to find someone who can hold an intelligent conversation. But luckily the U of C has more than its share of bright students, and Priya is one of the brightest."

Priya simpered at Ben, making Jessica feel even more ill.

"I met Priya in my Dostoyevsky class. I'll never forget the day when Pri corrected the TA; she reminded him that *A Disgraceful Affair* had been published before *The Dream of a Ridiculous Man,* not after."

"Disgraceful *and* Ridiculous. I'm so happy for you both." Jessica crossed her arms and scowled. *Dosta—who?* she wondered silently. *Did Priya turn Ben into a total snob? Or did he do it all by himself?*

"Don't tell me you haven't heard of him," Priya remarked loftily, her tone rising in disbelief. "Fyodor Mikhaylovich Dostoyevsky is an *essential* Russian author. Surely you've heard of his classics—*Notes from the Underground, The Devils?*" She shook her head as if totally amazed.

Jessica stared back blankly, her mind churning. *So what if I've never heard of this Russian guy or his books?* she wanted to yell. *I know a lot of other things*—important *things.* But for some reason the words wouldn't come out.

Priya sighed loudly. "What do they teach you at your little school?" She scanned Jessica from head to toe. "Makeup 101?"

"No." Jessica's eyes turned to slits as she examined Priya's smug face thoroughly; the makeup police needed to take Priya in and book her for heavy use of blush and eyeliner. "But *you* could sure use a class like that. Maybe I could give you a few tips . . . no, it'd all be a waste."

Priya's face darkened. "You've *got* to be kidding," she snarled. "What could *you* possibly teach *me*? If I were you, I'd be worrying about what's inside my head and not on my face!"

"Well, you're *not* me—"

"That's right," Priya cut in quickly. "At least I have an IQ that's higher than room temperature."

Jessica gasped and paled. She looked to Ben for backup. *How can he let her say something like that?* she wondered. *That was too low.*

To Jessica's horror, Ben chuckled. "I'm experiencing a sheer moment of schadenfreude right now."

"Speak English," Jessica growled.

"Let me translate for you," Priya purred. "Schadenfreude is a German term. It means taking joy in other people's misery."

"You . . . you—," Jessica sputtered.

"Jessica, Ryan is calling you," Ben interrupted. "I think he wants you back at your post. It's time for you to leave anyway."

"Good-bye, Jennifer," Priya sang in a poisonously sweet voice, holding up her hand and daintily wiggling her fingers.

Without a word Jessica spun around and tore across the beach toward Tower 2. Ben and Priya's cutting, cruel laughter followed her all the way there.

76

Chapter Five

"Where am I?" Nina croaked. She had just felt a big bump beneath her. She coughed, a noise that sounded strangely weak and hoarse to her own ears. Foggily she fluttered her eyes open. Her inner tube was half in the water and half in the sand. She tried sitting up and immediately had to lie back down. Blinking, Nina tried to focus; she was surrounded by what appeared to be miles of unfamiliar, deserted beach. It was eerily silent.

I must have fallen asleep, she realized, anxiety pumping through her veins. *I have absolutely no idea where I am.*

Even though the sun beat down relentlessly, Nina was suddenly aware that she was very cold. At the same time she was sweating heavily, her suit and jacket clinging like plastic wrap. Nina moaned as she tried to take a deep breath; it was too draining, and she was too exhausted.

Slowly Nina forced herself in an upright position and tried to climb out of the inner tube. But the world began to spin around her, sending her back down again. Icy surf splashed around her feet. Nina strained to scan the area and suddenly did a double take.

I must be seeing things, Nina thought, massaging her forehead. About a hundred yards away an enormous beach house loomed. The huge white adobe structure was nestled onto a rocky ledge overlooking the sea. Docked in front of the place was a sleek motorboat. Several surfboards were propped up under a striped cabana. Squinting, she noticed a curving driveway with a shining pewter-colored convertible VW Bug parked at the top.

What is this—some weird sort of Treasure Island? Or maybe I've stumbled onto Gilligan's Island and Ginger will stroll out to greet me. Nina shook her head as if to clear it. "Careful," she mumbled to herself. "You're totally losing it. You'd better close your eyes again and open them—slowly."

"Hey, how's it going?"

The strange voice made her jump. She struggled to sit up, but her arms were too weak to support her. She shaded her eyes with her hands and saw a tall, slender man standing over her. He was tightly muscled and very tanned, with longish, sun-streaked tawny hair. His face was chiseled, and his eyes were bluer than the sea itself. His expression was kind, not threatening in the least. Judging from his faded cutoffs, bare chest, and bare feet, he was obviously some young, hippified beach bum who lived only to wax his board and listen to the Grateful Dead.

"Wow, this is so gnarly," the man said in a pleasant, mellow voice. He knelt beside her, his blue, blue eyes only inches from hers. "But once I saved that dolphin from a fishing net, I knew the ocean would be sending me something in return."

"What?" Nina whispered hoarsely as the world around her began to spin. In an attempt to stop it, she focused on a black mark on the man's left bicep. *Is that a tattoo?* she wondered, befuddled. *Didn't I say something to someone about a tattoo the other day? Who was it? I . . . I can't remember.*

"Of course, I never counted on getting a mermaid as my thank-you present," he continued with a smile.

Nina rubbed her eyes. "What?" she demanded weakly.

"Karma," the man explained quietly, still smiling. "I don't know if you've ever heard of it—"

Nina reached out a hand. She had to stand

and get out of this inner tube—*now*. "This . . . this is crazy."

He caught her hand. "Hey, are you hungry? Do you wanna get something to eat?"

The last thing Nina saw was the man's face furrow with concern as she plunged into total darkness.

"You can trust me," Winston said persuasively, hoping his pasted-on smile hid his nervousness. The woman sitting on the other side of the desk stared owlishly at him, making him fidget. She hadn't blinked, Winston was sure, for about ten minutes. But maybe it was her appearance that made him uncomfortable.

Mavis Limgudder, manager and part owner of the Frost-ee-Freez Ice Cream and Novelty Company, strongly reminded Winston of a chainsmoking troll—the miniature doll kind. She was small and stout with a tower of raspberry-pink-tinted curls and huge horn-rimmed bifocals. Her cheeks were so rouged, they looked severely sunburned.

Winston cleared his throat. The office was tiny, hot, and smoky, and Ms. Limgudder was practically hidden behind mountains of papers and magazines. Behind her hung a giant framed print of an ice cream cone. The floor around her desk was almost completely covered with boxes and bags of undisclosed items.

I wonder how she gets out from behind her desk, Winston wondered. *There's no room for her to walk. Maybe she's a great long jumper.* The image of Ms. Limgudder in a hot pink, rhinestone-studded sweat suit sprinting across her junk-filled office made Winston want to laugh. But he swallowed the impulse. He needed this job desperately.

"Well, Mr. Egbert," Ms. Limgudder said in her gravelly voice after a long, agonizing minute. "Being a representative of Frost-ee-Freez is a big job. A very big job. My son—Sonny—is part owner too, and he takes his profits very seriously." She paused, lighting up another cigarette to add to the mound of smoldering butts in front of her.

Winston fought back a cough even though the smoke was irritating his sinuses. *Great,* he thought tensely. *Mavis sounds like she and her family are part of some kind of mob or something. Just what I need after that gambling disaster with Hamburger Harry's last summer.* Winston had eagerly and foolishly fallen in with Harry's scheme of collecting bets for the merit-pay contest between South Beach and Sweet Valley Shore. Winston had known deep down it was wrong, but the money and excitement had fogged his brain.

81

Winston sighed softly and pushed his glasses up with one finger. *Just remember,* he told himself, *you need this money for all those little extras while you're at SVU—especially those little extras for Denise. You love spending on Denise. You adore spending on Denise. Denise is worth a million little extras.*

Denise Waters was Winston's girlfriend and also the most beautiful woman at SVU and in the world, in his opinion. Winston wanted to wine her and dine her the way she deserved, even if she wasn't the materialistic type.

"So, Mr. Egbert," Ms. Limgudder rasped loudly, waking Winston from his fantasy. She held his résumé between two tobacco-stained fingers of one hand and her cigarette in the other. "Says here you're licensed as a commercial driver."

Winston flinched. "Uh, yes, I am," he squeaked, trying to smile.

"No, you're not," Ms. Limgudder retorted, glaring at him as she let his résumé drop down to the top of her desk. "I'm thorough and I checked. You're not commercially licensed at all." She carefully smashed her cigarette into the ashtray.

Winston felt his face heat up. "Well, you see— um—I'm a very good driver, and I figured . . ." His voice trailed off under Ms. Limgudder's fierce gaze.

That's it. I've blown it, Winston thought in despair. *I'm sorry, Denise.*

Something cold and wet was dripping on Nina's face. A trickle of water slid into her mouth. "Hey," she gasped, coughing. Nina opened her eyes and closed them again. *I'm still dreaming,* she told herself. Her would-be savior was patting her face and neck with a damp, cool cloth, his blue eyes dark with concern.

"You'll be OK soon," he told her, gently placing the cloth on her forehead. "You just had too much sun." He got up and pulled a floor fan closer. The breeze from the whirling blades felt good on Nina's warm face.

Nina looked around in disbelief and then stared down at herself. She was draped in moist, cool towels and lying on a large thick cushion on the floor. Her gaze swept the enormous, stark, pale blue octagonal room around her. It held little furniture, only a small table and one chair and a couple of glazed pottery pieces filled with plants. A bizarre-looking metal sculpture graced the table. The walls were covered with strange art, most of it in shades of maroon and ivory. A single round curtainless window overlooked the sea.

"Where am I?" Nina demanded, plucking the cloth from her forehead. "And what's this?" She thumped the mat beneath her.

The stranger smiled serenely and sat down beside her in a contorted, inhuman-looking position. "You're in my house, and you're lying on my *zaniku*."

"Huh?" Nina forced herself to sit up, her damp ponytail swaying with the movement. "What is a zan . . . zan . . . whatever?"

"*Zaniku*. It's where I meditate," the man explained. "You were out for the count, so I carried you in here. This room was the closest."

"Oh no," Nina moaned. "I was unconscious?" She peeked at the stranger from under her lashes; he was sitting with his eyes half shut and a slight smile on his lips. Nina shivered.

It looks like this weirdo has carried me off to his lair, Nina realized, glancing around the room again. *But this place can't be his.* She could tell the paintings were expensive and remembered how palatial the house looked when she woke up on the beach. *He's so scruffy. He can't possibly live here,* she thought, vaguely recalling the luxurious boat and vintage car outside. *Maybe he works here. Or maybe he's a drifter who's just broken into the place.*

Nina was suddenly, violently unsettled. She'd actually lost consciousness in front of this total stranger! She hated not being in control. Nina stared the man down, wishing he would go away and leave her alone.

"I'm Stu Kirkwood," the stranger announced, reaching over to take her hand in his. He gently squeezed it, his fingers briefly covering hers. "Are you feeling any better?"

"Let go of me." Nina jerked her hand back defensively. *He must be totally nuts,* Nina thought, frowning. *He acts like we've just met at a charming little social engagement instead of by some freak accident.*

"Hey, don't get uptight. Everything's cool." Stu smiled and brushed back a lock of sun-streaked hair from his forehead. "I forgot something in the kitchen. I'll be right back." Stu untwined himself from his contorted position and went out of the room.

Nina caught her breath, imagining that what he had forgotten was a large meat cleaver or at least a nasty-looking can opener. But when she tried to get up and escape, she had a dizzy spell and dropped back down onto the *zaniku.* The wet towels had fallen off her swimsuit-clad body, and she started replacing them, not wanting Stu to see that she had tried to run off when he came back in.

"The keys," she whispered. Nina had a set of keys to the beach house in the waterproof pocket of her lifeguard jacket; she could arrange them in her fist and strike at him if he tried anything funny. But she realized with dread that

Stu had apparently removed her jacket when she was unconscious. It was draped over the chair on the other side of the room, out of reach.

I can't believe this. Another classic Egbert foul-up, Winston thought miserably as he sat in a daze in Ms. Limgudder's office. *She's probably going to prosecute me for false advertising or whatever. I'll spend the whole summer in the slammer—*

The snapping of chubby fingers brought Winston to his senses. "Are you awake, Mr. Egbert?" Ms. Limgudder asked. "Our representatives have to be sharp and lively if they're going to survive in *this* business." She cackled and then started coughing and wheezing.

Winston gaped at her. *"Survive?"*

"That's right," she choked, gasping wildly.

"Hey, are you OK?"

"I'll be terrific in just a second," she said hoarsely. She lit another cigarette and took a deep drag. "Ah, just what I needed."

Winston resisted the urge to gag. "So, Ms. Limgudder, about the job . . ."

"You're hired," she said calmly. "You're a liar—but I happen to like that in a person." She winked at him. "If you keep your nose clean and stay out of trouble, everything should be fine. In this business you learn to cut corners."

Winston gulped. *In this business? She's got to be talking about the ice cream business, right?*

"Only one more thing we gotta take care of," Ms. Limgudder announced. "You gotta go next door for your fitting."

Winston gawked at her again. "My *fitting?*"

"For your Frost-ee-Freez uniform," she growled impatiently, motioning him to the door. "Oh yeah," she called before Winston shut the door behind him. "And welcome aboard. Hope you last longer than the last guy did."

Winston groaned as he headed slowly next door. He wondered briefly if he should make a break for the nearest exit. *Chin up, Egbert,* he reassured himself weakly. *Nothing could possibly be worse than the Hamburger Harry costume.*

When Stu reentered the room, Nina jumped instinctively. She grabbed the cushion that had been under her feet and held it in front of her for protection. But she heaved a sigh of relief when she saw that all he had brought with him was a big silver mixing bowl and spoon. *He could hardly do any serious damage with* that, Nina realized. She lay back down, just to be cooperative. She didn't want to do anything to make him angry.

"That's the *zafu*," Stu said good-naturedly, taking the cushion and putting it back under her feet. "It goes on the *zaniku,* usually. Since you'd passed out, I used it to get your circulation going to your head." After delicately putting the wet towels back in place, he sat down on the floor and began devouring what looked like half a box worth of cereal. He paused and held out the spoon. "Want some?"

Nina shook her head. "*Ab*-solutely *not,* Stu," she said quickly, grimacing with disgust.

"No sweat." Stu shrugged and resumed eating. "Hey," he suddenly exclaimed, setting the bowl on the floor. "I bet I know what you want instead." He sprang up and jogged out of the room.

What's he bringing now? Nina wondered, feeling her pulse accelerate. *A chain saw?* She watched the doorway, wishing she were strong enough to make a run for it. Then she looked wildly around her for any possible weapon close at hand. *That mixing bowl looks kind of heavy—*

Stu reappeared, carrying a small bottle of water. He handed it to Nina, cautioning, "Sip it slow," before he dropped gracefully down on the floor, his legs twisted pretzel-like. He picked up his bowl and resumed eating.

Nina watched him suspiciously. *This guy is a total wacko,* she decided. *He acts like people wash up on his beach every day.* "How can you sit like that?" she asked, curiosity getting the best of her.

Stu's eyes widened in mild surprise. "I always

sit in the lotus position. It's totally comfortable."

Nina examined the bottle of water carefully. She was dying of thirst, but who knew what he might have put into it? At least the seal was unbroken. Still, when Stu wasn't looking, she sniffed it before drinking. The water felt like heaven to her parched throat. Almost to her disappointment, she was feeling better and stronger by the second.

"You must use a killer sunscreen," Stu remarked. "Your face, legs, and hands don't show any signs of sunburn. What brand is it?"

"Uhhh . . . Tropibalm Select," Nina replied, looking down at her legs and hands. They were an only slightly richer cocoa color than her arms. "SPF 96."

"Wow. I'll have to check that stuff out."

Nina sat silently in thought while Stu wolfed down his cereal. *Thank goodness for that sunscreen,* Nina told herself. *How stupid was I, falling asleep like that? I could've been burned to a crisp. I could've drowned. I could've—*

"Until now I'd been feeling really bummed," Stu said, interrupting her thoughts. "There's been nothing but flat water or mush out in the ocean. I haven't been on my board in almost three days." He rubbed his jaw with a tanned hand and set the bowl down on the floor.

"So why didn't you spend your time meditating?" Nina snapped, annoyed that the guy wouldn't keep his mouth shut while she was trying to recover. "I thought your type was always *one with the universe* and that kind of thing."

Stu's clear blue eyes brushed her face, but he didn't seem insulted. "You're right, I shouldn't let the aggro get me, or I'll never reach Nirvana." He paused to eat a mouthful of cereal and nodded. "I'm still a student of Buddha."

Nina bit back a growl. "Do you *mind* telling me what you're talking about? How is water mushy? And if by aggro you mean aggravation, why don't you just say it? Are you intentionally trying to bug me?"

Stu's expression was unruffled. "I'm not trying to be mysterious or some sort of poser. Sometimes I just forget that not everyone lives for surfing. Mush is when the waves are breaking in all directions, and you're right—aggro is when something is aggravating, which I guess is what you think I am." Stu grinned for a second, his teeth flashing white against his golden brown skin.

Nina refused to respond. She continued sipping from her bottle of water. Her eyes drifted to the tattoo she'd noticed before she passed out. On his left bicep a small yin and yang symbol was rendered in black ink. Surrounding the tattoo was smooth skin and taut muscles—lots of muscles. Nina gulped her water faster.

Stu leaned forward to massage one of his muscular, defined calves, causing Nina to spit out a few drops of water. "Hey, not too fast, mystery girl," he said, patting her on the back gently. "By the way, what's your name?"

"None of your business!" *I can't believe this,* she thought, outraged as she scanned Stu a second time. *He's tall, muscular, and has gorgeous calves and a tattoo. This has to be some kind of joke. A* cosmic *joke.*

"That's cool with me," Stu said, clearly unoffended. "You'll tell me your name when you're ready. I'm not hung up on labels."

Nina rolled her eyes. "I hate those Zen-like statements. They drive me crazy."

"I'm sorry about that," Stu said quietly. "But I really try to live by it, you know?"

"People always brag about having values," Nina retorted bitingly, letting the water bottle drop to the floor. "But talk is cheap." She gave Stu a pointed look as she peeled the damp towels away from her swimsuit-clad body. *There, that's better,* she thought despite experiencing a moment of light-headedness.

"Life doesn't have to be like that. But I can't change your mind," Stu replied calmly. "You'll have to discover the truth for yourself."

"Nice cop-out," Nina quipped. She got up on her knees. "Look, Stu—if that *is* your real name—I need to know how I can get back to Sweet Valley Shore and—"

"Why shouldn't Stu be my name?" he interrupted her, a curious light in his eyes.

"Well, look at all this," Nina said, waving her hand around. "Do you really live here or what?"

Stu leaned forward, his gaze meeting Nina's dead-on. "Sure, I do." Despite the intensity in his eyes, he seemed confused.

"What you're really saying is that you *work* here, right?" Nina persisted. *C'mon, no guy who dresses and acts like this is going to own this kind of spread,* she thought in disbelief. "If you are who you say you are, let's see some ID."

Stu stared at her for a heartbeat and then got to his feet. He jammed his hand into the back pocket of his cutoffs and pulled out a wallet. Silently he handed Nina his driver's license. Stu Kirkwood's face smiled back at her. All his vital stats were listed, including his height: six-foot three.

Six-foot three! Omigosh, Nina thought in shock. She staggered to her feet, her head spinning. *The ideal height.* His address was listed as SeaMist Island with a post office box in Sweet Valley Shore. *This is an island!* Nina gasped silently, shaking as she reread the license. *He really lives on a deserted island!*

92

She couldn't bear to look Stu in the eye. She felt naked, as if he'd read her most private thoughts out loud. She was tempted to hurl the license back in his face but made herself hand it back carefully.

"Fine, I read it," she snarled. She could feel the blood heating her face as she struggled to control her rapid breathing. Stu pocketed the license and sat back down. He picked up his bowl, and for a second the only sound was him munching his cereal.

Nina tapped her foot. "Look, Stu, *you* may live here, but I *don't*. I have to get back *now*."

"No problem, little mermaid. I'll get you back home."

"Little mermaid!"

"Well, that's what you looked like when I fished you out of the water," Stu answered playfully.

Nina narrowed her eyes at Stu and scowled. *Just look at him,* she thought in disgust, *sitting on the floor and staring up at me with his big bowl of kibble in front of him. He's just begging to be petted. Well, he can forget it. I know a dog when I see one.*

Chapter Six

"No more shop talk," Elizabeth vowed cheerfully, slipping her arm through Ryan's as they made their way to the front entrance of the building where Patti lived. "Let's just kick back and both enjoy ourselves. We deserve it." She squeezed his arm, enjoying the feel of his hard muscle beneath her hand. Palm trees surrounding the old red brick apartment complex waved and danced in the balmy breeze. The sun was sinking against the sky in a blaze of brilliant color.

"You know, you're right, Elizabeth," Ryan replied casually. "I could use a little R and R." His gold-flecked eyes searched Elizabeth's before he bent down and brushed his lips against hers. "I was just thinking, maybe we should spend the evening together . . . alone." He kissed her again, a little more insistently. "We could always make up some excuse to leave early."

Elizabeth punched him lightly on the arm. "Spoilsport! You don't want to disappoint Patti, do you?"

Ryan sighed and gave her a sheepish smile. "You're right. Patti's waiting. Let's go." He pushed the intercom button next to a small card that read Yager, and they were immediately buzzed in.

Seconds later, after climbing to the second-floor apartment, they found Patti waiting for them. "Hi, you two!" she said, grinning broadly as she beckoned them in. Patti's red hair framed her face with wild curls, and her eyes were gleaming. "Wait until you see the dinner I've got planned."

I'm glad I dressed up, Elizabeth thought in relief as she smoothed down the skirt of her blue-and-pink-flowered sundress. Patti was wearing a pale green silk off-the-shoulder shirt, yellow shantung capri pants, and coordinating mules. Dangling shell earrings and a matching necklace completed her festive outfit.

"Have a seat," Patti urged, nodding toward the handsome, heavyset man lounging in a re-cliner. "You've both met Arthur."

Arthur held up a can of orange soda. "Cheers, you two. Glad you could stop by." Soft reggae music played in the background as

Elizabeth noted to herself that the furnishings in the apartment were casual and comfortable. The pale blue overstuffed sofa and matching easy chair looked particularly inviting.

"I like your apartment," Elizabeth said, smiling at both of the Yagers. "It's so cozy and warm. It reminds me of the Trail's End Pub."

Arthur beamed and held up his can of soda again. "Here's to the Trail's End, which is finally out of the red and into the black."

"Here, here," Ryan chimed in.

"And let's hope our good luck continues," Patti said cheerfully. She was standing behind Arthur's chair, her arms looped around his shoulders. "Arthur's been working day and night to keep his bar afloat. I hardly ever see him anymore." She kissed the top of his head.

"Hey, why don't you two have a seat?" Arthur suggested.

"Thanks," Ryan replied, cupping Elizabeth's arm and leading her to the couch. As they settled in among a collection of bright yellow and navy throw pillows, Ryan said, "I'm glad the pub is doing so well, Arthur. If anyone deserves a break, you and Patti do. Especially after all you've done for me."

Patti giggled. "Uh-oh, we're starting to get a little sentimental here. I'd better get the hors d'oeuvres."

After Patti disappeared into the kitchen, Ryan and Arthur fell into a discussion about local environmental laws. Elizabeth, who was an ardent activist herself, joined in eagerly.

"Chow's here!" Patti sashayed back into the living room, bearing a giant silver tray. Elizabeth started to get up to help her, but Patti was already shoving magazines off the coffee table. She dropped the tray down with a flourish.

"Just in time," Arthur commented, patting his solid stomach. "I was starting to feel faint."

Me too, Elizabeth realized when her stomach growled. The food smelled absolutely delicious. Filling the tray from end to end were tiny crab puffs, stuffed shrimp, chicken wings, tortilla chips and salsa, cheese dip, and a miniature French bread neatly sliced; everything had been placed on paper doilies or arranged in tiny dishes.

"Dig in and don't be shy," Patti urged, leaning over the table to grab a crab puff. "Dinner won't be ready for about forty-five minutes, so you might as well fill up."

"I won't be shy," Ryan assured her with a slight smile. He loaded up a plate with goodies and handed it to Elizabeth while Patti hurried back into the kitchen. "Ladies first," he teased affectionately.

Elizabeth blew him a kiss. "You know the

way to a girl's heart," she said before taking a bite of stuffed shrimp. It was spicy and rich. "Mmm, delicious," Elizabeth breathed as she took another look around the Yagers' apartment. *It's so sweet and homey,* Elizabeth thought. *Maybe Ryan and I will be living like this someday.* A warm feeling spread through her stomach, and it wasn't caused by the spicy shrimp.

"Anyone thirsty?" Patti called out gaily. "We've got everything, so I'm taking requests." Smiling casually, Patti reappeared in the living room, a bottle of beer in her hand. She held it up. "Anyone want one of these?"

Elizabeth froze, shock coursing through her veins. She recognized the brand; it wasn't non-alcoholic. *I hope she didn't buy that for* me, she thought in horror. After all, Patti wasn't only Ryan's A.A. sponsor; she was a recovering alcoholic herself. "No, thank you, Patti," Elizabeth said quickly.

Patti dangled the bottle in the air tantalizingly. "Ryan? How about you?"

Elizabeth's jaw nearly dropped to the floor.

"So tell me about your boyfriend, Miranda." Jessica leaned her elbows on a glossy red table in the Sip and Page Café. She and Miranda had driven all the way to Burkridge to find it.

Miranda took a bite of her almond biscotti

and shrugged. "Tony? He's an American studies major, like me. He's sweet, but it's really nothing serious. I don't know . . . I guess I have more fun just playing the field. Mmm, look at *that* one."

Jessica looked in the direction Miranda was indicating, but she couldn't tell which guy she meant. The truth was, there were tons of gorgeous guys at the Sip and Page. Lots of tan, young people milled about the café area. The bookstore section looked just as busy. The fragrant aroma of espresso mingled with the vanilla scent of cookies and scones. Classical violin music accompanied the soft murmur of voices. Some people were reading newspapers and magazines, while others talked and laughed as they sipped their drinks. It looked like the perfect place to meet someone new.

Sighing, Jessica stared down through the foam of her mochaccino. *Dark and cloudy, just like my life,* she thought sadly. *In a way, a cup of coffee is just like a guy. It looks so sweet, but it can turn out to be totally bitter.*

"Hunk alert at two o'clock, Jess," Miranda breathed. "And he's coming your way!" She gently nudged Jessica's foot under the table.

Jessica glanced discreetly across the room. An attractive dark-haired guy carrying a tall cup of coffee was coming toward their table. He paused for a moment as his eyes met Jessica's. His face seemed to brighten, but his expression fell as Jessica turned her eyes back to her mochaccino.

He's just not my type, Jessica thought glumly, rubbing the toe of her sandal-clad foot against the parquet floor. *He doesn't have incredible blue eyes and an asymmetrical killer smile. Besides, I don't want a guy who just likes me for my looks. I want one who appreciates my mind too.*

Miranda arched her brows; her eyes followed Jessica's admirer with an obvious expression of regret. "Too bad. He was a hottie. And he was *definitely* interested in you."

"Why is it that it's always the wrong guy who likes me?" Jessica moaned. She took a tiny drink of her mochaccino so she wouldn't have to answer. "Anyway," Jessica said, trying to distract herself. "We were talking about you."

"No, we were talking about guys," Miranda argued as she poured more sugar into her latte. "Now, if I can just lure one of those cuties around here over to *my* side."

It's like the song says, Jessica thought, unable to concentrate on the conversation. *Love stinks.*

"Now take that big, husky redhead, Jessica. He's a total babe—just my type," Miranda confided. "He's standing right by the business magazines, which is a good sign."

Jessica couldn't hold it in any longer. "I just don't get it!" she burst out. "What in the world does Ben *see* in her?"

"Whoa!" Miranda held up her hand. "Calm down, Jess. Don't forget, I have to *live* with Priya, remember?"

"I know it," Jessica muttered. "I don't see how Ben can stand being around Miss Brainiac, that's all."

Miranda looked pensive. "I don't know Ben as well as you do, Jess. But it seems to me that Ben is the kind of guy who likes a challenge." Miranda inched her chair closer. "From what you tell me, Ben is totally into mental stimulation, and I bet you *anything* that Priya uses that to her advantage. I'll have to say this for the little snot—she *is* smart."

Jessica frowned and tapped a glossy nail on the table. "Well, I can be smart too, you know. Just because I don't go around showing off doesn't mean I don't know as much as she does." Jessica tugged at the hem of her purple minidress. "It's not like Priya is the only one who can read about this Dusty—Dusta—whoever he is!"

"Dostoyevsky," Miranda corrected with a grin. "You're right, Jess. You're not only smart, but you're much cleverer than Priya. You'd probably like Dostoyevsky too. He's a great writer."

"Yeah . . . that's it!" Jessica cried out, suddenly struck with inspiration. "That's the answer." She sprang to her feet and swung her purse over her shoulder. "C'mon, Miranda."

Miranda gulped the last of her latte and clambered to her feet. "Where are we going?"

"We're going to find some of those Derstumnevsky books. I'll show Ben who the *real* Einstein is around here."

Is this a test? Elizabeth wondered as she watched Patti hold up the beer, her eyebrows raised, clearly waiting for Ryan's response. *No. It can't be. This is some kind of weird joke.*

Elizabeth turned to Ryan for a sign of what was going on. His face was hard as stone, his eyes dark and cold. "No, Patti," was all he said.

This is no test, Elizabeth realized. *This is no joke. This is real.*

Patti shrugged blithely. "Arthur? Want one?"

"I've got mine, honey," he replied, holding up his can of orange soda.

"Oh, well." Patti sighed as she cracked open the beer and took a swig. "Ryan, Liz, we've got whatever you're in the mood for, so come help yourselves."

Elizabeth couldn't help herself. She was paralyzed, unable to take her eyes off Patti as she continued to sip from her beer bottle. *Why doesn't anyone say something?* Elizabeth wondered urgently as her stomach sank to the floor. *This is like watching someone drowning. And none of us are doing a thing about it!*

"We'll just have a Coke," Ryan said, his voice free of emotion. "I'll get them." Before he stood up, he put a cautioning hand on Elizabeth's quivering wrist. The gesture seemed to say, *I know what you're thinking. Let me handle this.* But after he followed Patti into the kitchen, he came back almost immediately with the sodas. He obviously hadn't said a word to her.

As Elizabeth grabbed her can from him she whispered, "What's going on?"

Ryan refused to meet her eyes. "Just leave it, OK?" he hissed back. "Let's just have a good time, like you said." He shot a glance at Arthur, who seemed oblivious and immersed in his food.

A good time? Elizabeth echoed to herself. *Watching Patti self-destruct? Her drinking—that must be the thing that's been weighing on Ryan's mind lately, and with good reason. But how could he not think this would affect me too?*

Elizabeth set her plate of half-eaten food onto the table and clasped her hands tightly. Anything to stop herself from leaping up and dragging Ryan out the door.

103

Ryan was busily eating. *Or at least, he looks like he's busy eating,* Elizabeth fretted. *Who knows what's going on in his head? I can't imagine how difficult this is for him. He must be struggling harder than ever to stay sober.* Elizabeth shot him a tense look from under her eyelashes. *Why couldn't he tell me this himself? Is there something else going on that I don't know about?*

With that thought Elizabeth felt icy dread crawl up her spine, and she shivered.

Jessica raced down the ramp that connected the Sip and Page Café to the bookstore with Miranda at her heels. She panted as she wove her way past New Age, Your Money, and Inner Beauty. Finally she found Classical Fiction. She skimmed through the racks until she found the *D*s and Dostoyevsky, her pointing finger trembling with excitement. "Aha!"

"You're not going to buy all his stuff, are you?" Miranda asked, eyes wide with disbelief.

"Get real. I'm not going to waste my entire summer reading." Jessica yanked out a few books and read the titles, some of which sounded vaguely like the ones Priya had mentioned.

"Let's see," Jessica muttered. "The guys on the cover of *The Brothers Karamazov* are totally not cute, so the book is probably superboring.

104

The Idiot"—she snickered—"that must be Priya's life story."

Miranda giggled over her shoulder. "No, her book would be called *The Egomaniac*."

Jessica shoved the volumes back onto the shelf. "Wait," she said, tapping the spine of another book. "Here's something called *The Double*—maybe it's about twins." Her eyes lit up with interest.

"Uh, I don't think so, Jess," Miranda warned. "That's not one I've read, but—"

"Never mind that," Jessica interrupted excitedly. "Look!" She pulled out a book. "This one's called *Crime and Punishment*! I bet that's just like *Criminal Justice*, which in my humble opinion is the best show on TV."

"I don't know. . . ."

"The guy who plays the renegade public defender is sooo fine." Jessica swooned. "This is the one. This is the key to making Ben sit up and take notice of me!" She held up *Crime and Punishment* proudly, as if it were a trophy.

"Well, if you say so." Miranda grinned. "My money's on you, Jess. Priya had better watch out. You can take her any day."

"I hope you're right, Miranda." Jessica ran a trembling hand over the smooth paperback cover and bit her lip. She pressed the book against her chest, feeling a little light-headed.

For some reason the book seemed to be getting heavier by the second. "All I can say is, this Russian guy must have written some pretty hot stuff. Why else would Ben fall for Priya? His books must be incredibly romantic."

Jessica smiled dreamily, her dimple flashing in her left cheek. "Just think what he'll do for me." She took a deep breath and whispered, "OK, Dusty—whatever, it's up to you now. My future is in your hands."

Chapter Seven

Why do I feel like I just swallowed a giant bowling ball? Ryan thought miserably as he cut into the juicy slice of roast beef on his plate. The faux-Tiffany lamp hanging overhead seemed far too bright; it shone in his eyes and made his head ache. He felt like a criminal who had been taken in for questioning.

I'm trapped, Ryan thought, trying to catch Patti's eye for what seemed like the hundredth time. *Patti's got to know she's making everyone uncomfortable.*

But his A.A. sponsor seemed perfectly fine; she served everything graciously and flawlessly and was making fine conversation. Even though she was on her fourth or fifth beer, she appeared to be totally in control.

In a way, I almost envy Patti, Ryan realized.

She's not worrying about anyone else's feelings. She's not agonizing about whether she's doing the right thing. She's not stressing out at all. Ryan took a forkful of potato, stared at it, and set it down. He had to admit the dinner was outstanding—the roast was perfection, the twice-baked potatoes mouthwatering, and the wild-mushroom dish delectable. *But it might as well be cardboard,* he thought miserably. *I can't eat anything.*

Ryan shot a look at Elizabeth, who was seated to his right. She was silently picking at her food and nodding at something Arthur was saying.

Her delicate profile was calm, her expression polite, but Ryan could read the unhappiness in her aqua eyes. *Her eyes always give her away,* he told himself. He wanted to apologize to her that second for putting her through this. But how could he?

"All right, everyone," Patti chirped, leaping to her feet. "It's dessert time! Wait until you see the pièce de résistance."

How does Patti do it? Ryan wondered, awestruck. *She's not even slurring her words.*

Ryan cleared his throat. "Uh, I'm pretty full. I'll skip dessert, if you don't mind."

"Me too," Elizabeth quickly chimed in, looking nervously at Ryan.

Ryan could read the message she was sending: *Let's get out of here.* Ryan sympathized with her feelings completely. But first he had to talk to Patti alone. He reached under the table and squeezed Elizabeth's limp hand. When she didn't respond, his heart lurched.

Arthur wiped his mouth with his napkin and set it calmly on the table. "I'll eat mine later, hon. I want to catch the news."

Arthur is amazing, Ryan thought, disgusted. *He doesn't seem to care that Patti's drinking again. Then again, in Elizabeth's eyes, I must not seem to care either.*

"Liz, why don't you join him," Ryan suggested. "I'll help Patti clean up." His eyes pleaded with hers.

Elizabeth's anxious glance went from Patti, who was clearing dishes, back to him. She nodded. "OK, but don't forget, I have a long day tomorrow. I really need to turn in early." She bit her lip and nodded slightly, as if to remind him that the evening was a total disaster.

Ryan twitched a little, his face hot with shame. "We won't stay late," he answered quickly. "Patti and Arthur are probably pretty tired too."

"Don't be silly, Ryan. The night's still young. Besides, I bought this gourmet cherry pie." She turned on the faucet and ran the

109

dishes under the water. "I even have vanilla ice cream to go with it. I guarantee you guys won't be able to resist once I bring dessert out."

Great, Ryan thought, watching as Elizabeth and Arthur left the kitchen. *Patti's so sensible and calm. This isn't going to be easy.* Sighing, Ryan gathered silverware and glasses and set them on the counter by the sink. In the meantime Patti had pulled another beer from the refrigerator.

Ryan took a deep breath. "Listen, Patti, we have to talk," he began, pointing to the bottle in her hand. "And this time I want you to really listen."

"Well, I don't want to hear it, Ryan," she replied gently but forcefully. "Like I've told you before, I know what I'm doing." She frowned at him and twisted off the bottle cap. She took a long slug and daintily wiped her mouth with her hand.

"You're getting out of control, Patti," Ryan said, breathing fast. "Can't you see how destructive you're being to yourself—and me?"

Patti slammed the bottle down on the kitchen counter and folded her arms across her chest. "Lighten up, Ryan," she said, her hazel eyes flashing. "Like I told you the *last* time you tried lecturing me, I know what I'm doing."

"You think you do—"

"I *know* I do," Patti corrected. "Those A.A. people would have you think that life is all black or all white. That you're either drunk or sober. Off the wagon or on it." She shook her head. "I refuse to live such a boring, uptight life. You *can* drink as long as it's in moderation."

Ryan's mouth went dry. He was feeling more panicky by the second. "That's totally wrong, Patti. You know what A.A. says—there's no such thing as drinking just a little. At least not for alcoholics."

Patti leaned forward. "They're wrong, and I know it. I've been drinking for a month now and look at me—I'm in total control."

"You're in denial."

"That's just bull," Patti snapped. Regaining her composure, she smiled. "Look, Ryan, I'm telling you the truth. You can live a normal life like everyone else. Why shouldn't you have a drink once in a while? You and I can both handle it. We've learned our lesson. We know when to stop."

"We *don't*, Patti, and that's the problem," Ryan hissed. "I figured that if I brought Elizabeth over, you'd at least show some respect and not show off like this. I guess I was wrong. How am I going to explain this to her?"

"Grow up. Elizabeth's not the one who's got a problem," Patti shot back. "*You* do because

111

you know I'm right. You *can* control alcohol, Ryan. You don't have to let it control you." Patti turned back to the kitchen sink and began scrubbing the dishes furiously.

Ryan walked out without saying another word. But right as he turned the corner into the living room, he heard the faint sound of breaking glass.

I'm finally free, Nina told herself, squirming impatiently as Stu backed his VW slowly down the long, winding driveway. She tightened her seat belt a notch just to be safe. *I don't think I can stand much more of Nature Boy's company.*

Stu was driving his convertible with no music playing, which to Nina seemed a little odd. Everyone liked tunes while they were driving.

Well, Stu would have to go and be unconventional. He's probably listening to the symphony of nature. Nina snorted quietly. The cool evening breeze wafted across her skin and sent her hair flying. She gazed out at the ocean as they drove across the bridge that connected the island to the mainland. The waves were getting wilder and bigger.

Stu claims he built the bridge himself. But where does a guy like him get that kind of money? Nina turned to stare hard at Stu, and he caught her looking at him. He responded with a sweet smile.

Nina sighed. It was almost impossible to insult the guy—and she'd been trying all day. He was just too puppy-doggy, too New Age for Nina. And besides he was a *guy*, which meant that no matter how much time he spent meditating, he was still male through and through—untrustworthy and unfaithful.

Stu had insisted that Nina spend the several hours resting on his *zaniku* while he fed her. She'd refused the weird-looking cereal but had given in and eaten Stu's homemade veggie soup and fresh honeydew. Stu kept taking her pulse and checking her stats as if he had been watching too many medical emergency dramas on TV. He told her over and over again that if she felt the least bit nauseous, he'd take her to the closest emergency room.

That would be a laugh, Nina thought. *I can just picture Zen Man conversing with the doctors and nurses. He'd probably start instructing them all on how to breathe and visualize healthy images.*

"So, little mermaid," Stu began lightly, "you're frowning. That's not good, you know. You don't want to draw all the negative vibes your way."

"For the last time stop calling me that," Nina said irritably. As annoying as the nickname was, the last thing she wanted to do was tell him her name. Why bother? She was never going to see him again.

"But it fits you," Stu insisted, grinning at her. "Seems like you and the water just naturally go together. You're both kind of wild."

"Hardly." Nina sighed loudly. "Like I told you, I work as a lifeguard. So yes, I do like the ocean. But I'm no mermaid!"

Stu's fair hair gleamed in the moonlight, and the muscles in his lean arms rippled as he expertly steered the VW. "I can see you protecting the water," he said, nodding wisely. "I sense that you're strong and vigilant, and that your spirit is very open and embracing too."

"I protect *people* who *swim* in the water."

"Same thing," Stu responded calmly. "Humans, animals, water, nature—we're all connected."

"Oh, puh-leeze," Nina burst out, whirling around to face him as much as the seat belt would allow. "Don't you ever stop with this touchy-feely stuff?"

But Stu didn't seem to be listening. The road they were on curved closer to the ocean, and Stu was looking raptly out at the surf. "Wow, get a load of the rip coming south! I've got to get my stick out tonight!"

"What language are you speaking *now?*"

Stu glanced quickly at her, his face lit up, his eyes glowing. "Those waves are totally perfect— uh, for surfing."

114

"Ohhh, I get it," Nina replied sarcastically. *Not that I can relate,* she thought. *I've never really surfed. Last summer Paul showed me a board, but that was about it.* Remembering Paul made Nina's jaw tighten.

Stu looked starry-eyed. "It's going to be totally juice out there." He smiled happily at Nina and turned the VW onto the main road toward Sweet Valley Shore. "This is my lucky day," he announced.

Nina sighed. Stu acted as if he were married to his surfboard, which he probably was. *I bet he's more faithful to his board than to any woman,* she thought cynically. *This guy and a big piece of wood—a match made in heaven.*

"Fyodor Dostoyevsky was born in 1821," Jessica read aloud, flipping back to the book's prologue. "*Eighteen twenty-one!* Well, no wonder I can't relate to anything Dusty says. He's too *old!*"

Suddenly Jessica knew that this night would go down in the record books as the most boring Friday night of her life. The second she had come back from Sip and Page, she'd found the house completely empty; everyone else must have gone out to have some actual fun. Jessica, however, immediately changed into her faded sweats and started reading *Crime and Punishment.* She'd been at it for nearly two hours and was almost proud of herself for sticking with such a dull task. *But it's no surprise my head is aching,* Jessica thought. *Whose wouldn't?*

Jessica tossed the book up toward the ceiling and flopped backward. *Is stealing Ben back from Priya really worth this agony?* she wondered, reaching for the book again. Jessica flashed back to Ben's heart-stopping kisses and needle-sharp wit and sank farther into the pillow. *OK, maybe it is, but still . . .*

"I don't get it," she went on, holding *Crime and Punishment* to her chest while talking to the ceiling. "A guy kills his landlady, and then he feels real bad about it. What's the big deal?"

Jessica impatiently turned a few pages. Her eyes backtracked suddenly to one particular passage in which a woman was dragging her husband around the room by his hair because he'd been out partying for days.

"Too bad Velcro Girl isn't here right now," she murmured, savoring a vision of herself hauling Priya around by her long black tresses. "This book is giving me ideas."

Sighing, she forced herself back into *Crime and Punishment*. But memories of Ben kept interrupting. Ben's bright blue eyes that seemed to look into her soul. Ben teasing her as he pretended to give her a pedicure at the beauty salon. Ben's strong arms holding Jessica close . . .

And now he's holding Priya. Well, not for long, she reminded herself. But when she gazed down at the book's text, her eyes blurred. "This is hopeless," she cried. "It's nothing like *Criminal Justice . . .*" Jessica sneaked a peek at the clock radio and grinned. ". . . which just happens to be on right now!"

Jessica popped up, dropped the book, and headed for the stairs. *Time for a study break,* she thought happily, relieved to leave Dostoyevsky behind. She grabbed a bag of blue corn chips and a soda from the kitchen and raced out to the living room. Smiling in anticipation, she jumped onto the striped canvas couch and hit the remote control.

In seconds she was blissfully lost in the story, snacking away contentedly. *A single minute of this show is a zillion times more exciting than Dusty's entire book,* she thought. *I mean, how many more pages do I have to go through before I get to the good stuff?*

"Listen, Stu. I am going to pay you back, I promise," Nina insisted as they drew nearer to Sweet Valley Shore. "You'll have to let me know how much the inner tube man charges you."

Nina couldn't even imagine what she'd be billed for having the inner tube out for almost an entire day. Since the inner tube man turned out to be a buddy of Stu's, he'd offered to smooth things over on her behalf. But Nina was proud. She took care of her own debts.

Stu raised an eyebrow. "Like, the money is really bugging you, isn't it?"

"Um, *yes*, it is. *I* may not be rich, but I don't like owing people."

Stu shook his head. "Someday you'll help someone else out. Then you won't owe a thing."

"You can't take karma to the bank, you know," Nina snapped. "The last time I checked, only ATMs supplied the green stuff."

"You don't understand. Karma can't be reduced to numbers," Stu insisted. "If you put the good energy out there, it will come back to you someday."

"Terrific, but I'm still paying you back—in cold hard cash."

Not answering, Stu suddenly slowed down and swerved to the side of the road.

"Why are we stopping?" Nina asked suspiciously.

"Look."

A tall, gnarled, ancient-looking bristlecone grew near the ditch, its thick, twisted roots visible through the dirt.

"That old guy is special," Stu said softly. "He reminds us of *tathata*—meaning he is a symbol that

118

the world is what it is. And we must accept it."

Nina studied the tree but remained silent. *OK, so the tree is obviously hundreds of years old and that's fine, but how can Stu read something so deep into shriveled-up wood?* She sighed. *I'll just ignore him—otherwise he'll get me totally confused.*

"No matter what you say, I'm giving you the money," Nina announced. "You can keep it or sprinkle it over all the trees in Tibet. I don't care."

"Don't worry. It will all work itself out."

What's the use? Nina decided. *Arguing with Stu is like boxing air.* Stu kept silent for several minutes, obviously lost in thought. *What a joke. A little tree hugging is all fine and good, but this is ridiculous.* She was overjoyed when he started driving again. Luckily the beach house was about a mile away, and Nina would finally be able to make her escape.

When they reached the house, it was silent and dark. Stu put the VW in park and turned toward Nina. "You're getting those dark vibes again." His blue eyes shone like stars.

Nina felt a tiny shiver slide up her spine. Her heart quickened a little. Nervously she reached for the car door handle. "Well, gotta go," she said in an unintentionally loud voice. "I've got an early shift tomorrow." Avoiding Stu's eyes,

Nina slid across the seat of the car and scrambled out. "I'll mail the money I owe you. And, uh . . . thanks for helping me when I was sick and everything."

Just before she slammed the door shut, Stu called out, "No problem, little mermaid. I'll be seeing you." His voice was warm and soft, almost a caress.

Not in this lifetime, Nina thought as she ran up the driveway to the house. She finally let herself relax when she heard the VW's motor rev up and the wheels peel out.

Unable to stop herself, Nina glanced over her shoulder and watched as Stu disappeared into the darkness. "Go back to your doghouse and stay, now," she murmured. "Good boy."

Chapter
Eight

"What the—," Elizabeth cried out in surprise as she stumbled in the sand. She bent down and scooped up the abandoned soda bottle she'd tripped over. It glistened in the bright sun.

"What happened?" Ryan asked urgently.

"I'm all right," she assured him quickly. "It's nothing, just a bottle." She threw it into the nearest recycling bin.

Elizabeth couldn't believe that Ryan had asked her to share Saturday-morning trash duty with him. Ever since they'd made a hasty retreat from the Yagers' place last night, neither she nor Ryan had brought up the touchy subject of Patti. The silence was uncomfortable but unbreakable; the beach was not the place to talk about Patti's backsliding, and the first big morning of the summer season was not the time.

"People are such pigs," Ryan snarled in disgust. "I'll have to talk to Theo. He was supposed to rake the beach last night and check for glass."

"It could have been left by someone who came after the beach was closed," Elizabeth suggested. "Or maybe a tourist. They don't always follow the rules."

"Don't make excuses for Theo, Elizabeth," Ryan snapped. "He's not doing his job."

Elizabeth bit back a sigh. As she looked for more hidden bottles she accidentally bumped into Ryan. "Sorry," she said automatically before turning to look at the ocean. The surf was wilder today, foaming and churning. The wave periods were faster, and greater swells were coming in. Elizabeth noted a few bodysurfers on their boogie boards and windsurfers taking advantage of the waves. Farther out past the jetty regular surfers were gliding on the bigger waves, looking almost as if they were flying.

Elizabeth sighed softly as she shielded her eyes to watch for a moment. *Those surfers are lucky. They're so carefree out there.*

"Elizabeth! Wake up!" Ryan called. His face looked dark, as if he were about to chastise her for turning her attention away from her duties for a few seconds.

"*What*, Ryan?"

"I'm going to put out the red flags. The water is way too dangerous." He strode into the tower supply room and returned with the flags. "I'm fastening down the swimming signs near the jetties and rocks too."

"I'll check for more glass," Elizabeth offered. She slipped inside the supply room and gathered a rake and garbage bag. It seemed unlikely, but if someone happened to cut themselves on a broken bottle, Ryan would go ballistic.

Elizabeth raked across the dunes but found only a few potato chip bags and candy wrappers buried in the sand. The wind was increasing, pulling at her ponytail. But in spite of the overcast sky and sharp winds, Sweet Valley Shore was filling up with people rapidly.

"All right!" a hearty voice bellowed. "Party time!" A chorus of whoops followed as a boom box exploded to life.

Several yards away a group of five college-age guys were throwing down towels and gathering around a plastic foam cooler. Two of them yanked off their Michigan State University T-shirts and slam-dunked them to the ground. The other three were laughing and slapping one another's hands as they cracked open a six-pack. A skinny guy with long dark hair that fell to his waist tilted his head back and began chugalugging to the cheers of his buddies.

123

Elizabeth felt her heart thump in dull, heavy strokes against her chest as she walked toward them. Approaching rowdies always made her a little nervous. *It's all part of my job,* she reminded herself, squaring her shoulders. *I'm in charge here, and it's up to me to protect everyone else on the beach.*

Slowly she approached the boisterous group. *Totally gross,* she thought in disgust. *Getting drunk in the morning. Well, getting drunk, period.*

"Hey, are you blind?" Ryan shouted, making Elizabeth jump as he came running up behind her. A vein pulsed in his forehead. "Can't you read the signs? No booze on the beach! Now move it or I'll move it for you."

Elizabeth's heart hammered triple time. *Please,* she prayed, *please don't let there be trouble.*

A tall beefy guy in striped shorts casually grabbed a can from the cooler and leered at Elizabeth. "Hey, we'll give up the beer if we can have her in exchange."

Elizabeth shot Striped Shorts an icy look, her hand itching to smack his face.

"I'd shut up if I were you," Ryan snarled. "Unless you want more trouble than you've already got." He took a step forward, and Elizabeth felt her lungs squeeze tightly.

The beefy guy glanced back at his buddies.

124

He smirked and deliberately took a long drink of beer.

Ryan glared at them icily. "If you want to do this the hard way, we can get the sheriff over here." Ryan jerked his head toward the GMC police truck that had just appeared on the far side of the dunes.

The skinny guy with long dark hair shrugged and stepped forward, kicking the cooler in Ryan's direction. "No problem, man," he said, though his eyes told a different story.

Sweat beads clung to Ryan's forehead. Without turning his head, he demanded through gritted teeth, "Elizabeth, take the cooler."

Swallowing hard, she stepped forward and hoisted up the cooler, biting back a groan. It felt as if it weighed a ton. *Why doesn't Ryan help me carry this thing?* she wondered, struggling to keep a grip on it. She hesitated, her fingers slipping as they dug harder into the plastic foam. "Uh, what should I do with it?" she asked, feeling foolish.

Ryan whirled on her, his face scarlet. "Just get rid of it! Get it out of my sight!" he barked. "Can't you just do your job, Liz?"

This stupid mustache, Winston thought, annoyed. *This stupid* fake *mustache.* The itchy hair kept drooping and falling into Winston's mouth. And it smelled weird, like mothballs. *I should just yank it off—but that would probably hurt. Mavis used a ton of glue on me.*

Winston steered the Frost-ee-Freez ice cream truck with one hand and used the other to brush the oversize handlebar mustache from his mouth. The truck swerved as if it had a mind of its own. *Great. This mustache is going to kill me. I just know it.*

"I'm such a wimp," Winston muttered, racked with self-disgust. "I should have stood up for myself." Winston couldn't suppress a chuckle as he pictured himself telling Ms. Limgudder off. *"Here,"* he would say grandly, throwing the fake mustache right into her lap. *"Wear it yourself!"* Winston guffawed even harder as he imagined the pink-haired Ms. Limgudder in a mustache. Suddenly the waistband of his pants strained and threatened to burst open.

"Awww, jeez," Winston moaned, his laughter vanishing. "Not only do I look like an idiot, but this stupid costume is too tight. I bet the Good Humor Man never had to dress like this. This is worse than being a hamburger."

Winston tugged at the front of the bubble-gum-pink-and-white-striped, old-fashioned linen suit. It was not only tight and too short, but extremely hot.

"What is this thing made out of? Thinsulate?" he asked his red-faced reflection in the rearview mirror. He felt like a turkey, bound in tinfoil, roasting slowly in an oven.

To top it all off, the giant, starched white bow tie was itchy and causing a red welt to form on Winston's skin. The white top hat was too big and kept dipping down over his brow. With his vision periodically obscured, Winston was forced to drive at a crawl. Cars beeped constantly at him as they passed by. They were probably laughing at him too.

I bet I look like Mr. Peanut, Winston decided. *A big, striped, psychedelic Mr. Peanut.*

Winston peered down at himself. "Mavis says I'm supposed to be a turn-of-the-century ice cream man," he said with a loud sigh. "But I look more like a turn-of-the-century jerk. Maybe I should reconsider—"

Suddenly a voice echoed through Winston's head. *"Big bonuses,"* Mavis had growled. *"You bring in a lot of business and you'll be making a lot of dough."*

All Winston's itches and other physical discomforts began to fade. Dollar signs danced in front of his eyes. He was reminded of something he'd read in Adam Smith's *Wealth of Nations* for his economics class: the more painful the job performed, the greater the compensation. If

127

that was true, he was sure to be a millionaire by the end of the summer. Money was money when it came down to it, and Winston needed every cent he could make for his beloved Denise. She was worth any amount of suffering.

Winston rubbed at the sweat trickling down his forehead. He jiggled the air-conditioning knob on the truck panel; nothing came out but a sickly, tepid wheeze. Winston sighed loudly. It was time to roll down the windows—and time to check the route that had been assigned to him.

While the truck lurched menacingly, Winston glanced at his official Frost-ee-Freez map, then turned left down Leland Street. Cruising through the residential area, Winston flipped the switch that sent calliope music blaring from the plastic loudspeakers. In less than two minutes kids descended on him from all sides, waving dollar bills in their hands.

Winston grinned as he stopped the truck and hopped out. *Look at all those cute little faces,* he thought. "Hi, kids," he called out cheerfully.

"Hi, Mr. Ice Cream Man," a tiny girl lisped, holding on to her mother's hand.

Winston went to the back and opened up the freezer. As he handed out ice cream sandwiches, fudge bars, juice bars, and other frozen confections as quickly as he could, Winston felt something warm and happy blossom inside him. *You know, I always admired the ice cream man when I was a kid,* Winston reminisced, handing a dinosaur-shaped Popsicle to a chubby-cheeked toddler. *Now I am the ice cream man. Cool!*

Climbing back into the truck, Winston peeked inside his cashbox. *Wow, what a haul,* he realized. *And I still have lots of streets to go to.* For a moment he almost forgot how uncomfortable he was.

I bet I've made more money than any other ice cream man around, Winston congratulated himself. *I've made a lot of little kids happy too.* He glanced down at his map and blinked. The grin faded from his face when he realized that he'd been routed right past Sweet Valley Shore. For a second he was tempted to skip it. Winston's friends would have a field day if they saw him in this getup.

Sighing, Winston steered the truck toward Sweet Valley Shore. *C'mon,* he reassured himself. *What are the odds of any of the lifeguards running after an ice cream truck?*

Ryan's harsh words echoed in Elizabeth's ears. Gasping, she stepped back and nearly stumbled in the sand. Acutely aware of the college guys gaping at her, she didn't say a word. She simply turned and headed back to the tower, struggling to contain her rapid breathing.

129

"What a guy, huh?" one of the guys remarked. "Lets his girlfriend do all the heavy work!"

Elizabeth hoped the footsteps running to her aid belonged to Ryan. Instead, when she turned, she saw Striped Shorts. "Hey, want some help?" he asked.

"No, thanks," she panted swiftly, every muscle tensing as Ryan appeared at her side.

"You're lucky I don't pitch you all off this beach," Ryan said through gritted teeth. "You can pick up your cooler when you leave."

"Whatever." The guy shrugged and strolled back toward his friends.

Elizabeth couldn't bring herself to look at Ryan. Her back felt as if it were on fire. She was about to let the cooler drop when without uttering a word, Ryan jerked it out of her arms. Swinging the container easily onto his shoulder, he barreled ahead. Elizabeth stopped in her tracks for a second and glared after Ryan's retreating back. "This has gone on long enough, Ryan Taylor," she muttered under her breath. "You and I are going to have it out once and for all."

Elizabeth reached the Main Tower right when Ryan disappeared inside with the cooler. Seconds later he was back.

"Look, Liz, I didn't mean to go off on you like that. I just—"

"Forget it." She looked around to make sure no one else was around to hear them. "Ryan . . . we really have to talk."

"I can't. Not right now." He looked aloof and assured in his reflector sunglasses with his arms crossed in front of him. But Elizabeth wasn't fooled; she could see his lips were in a tight line and his posture was too straight.

"We've got to talk this out," Elizabeth persisted. "I know you're worried about Patti, but something else is going on too. I can tell."

Ryan remained silent. Elizabeth put her hand on his arm gently. He felt stiff and lifeless.

"Please, Ryan. You can't go on pretending that nothing's wrong."

"Well, we can't discuss it here." Ryan ran an anxious, vaguely trembling hand through his sun-streaked curls. "Meet me at my place after work." He took off his sunglasses and rubbed his eyes.

"Ryan?"

"It's nothing," he said brusquely. "My contacts are bothering me."

Elizabeth shook her head. She could see the dark misery in his eyes. "If there's anything—"

"I'd better go check on those flags," he interrupted, replacing the sunglasses before sprinting off.

Elizabeth knew he was glad to get away from

131

her and her questions. Feeling hammered and drained, she went to pick up the rake but instead grabbed the pair of binoculars Ryan left behind. Bringing them to her eyes, she watched him walk along the ocean, his shoulders hunched, head down.

Ryan always keeps his eyes on the water, she thought in shock as she slowly put the binoculars down. *This is totally unlike him.* Trembling, Elizabeth felt something die inside her.

"Gross," Nina muttered under her breath as she peered angrily through her binoculars. It was oven hot and windy sitting at Tower 4, but Nina didn't notice; she was too intent on the scene about fifty yards away from her. A very well-built blond guy in baggy green trunks was hitting on a pretty redhead stretched out on a towel. The girl was smiling up at him and patting the towel beside her.

She wouldn't look so pleased if she knew he'd been kissing that brunette on a minibike a mere five minutes ago, Nina thought in disgust.

"Ugh," Nina said, putting the binoculars down on Theo's empty chair. "Maybe I should warn her." After all, she was here to protect the public from danger—and to Nina, that guy *definitely* qualified as a danger, or at least a nuisance.

Nina squinted at a bunch of kids who were wading out into the ocean and ignoring the No Swimming signs. Theo hurried over to the edge of the surf and blew his whistle for the kids to get back on the shore. Nina felt a pang of sympathy. Dealing with the public wasn't easy. With the water so rough today, Theo was out patrolling the more danger-prone areas. It seemed as if there were always swimmers ready to break the rules.

The binoculars were practically calling to her from Theo's chair; she couldn't resist. Eagerly Nina picked them up and beamed them back at the blond guy and his victim. He was rubbing suntan lotion onto the girl's back.

"What a player!" Nina muttered in outrage. "I should run down there and smack that smile off his—"

"Hey, there, little mermaid."

Nina jumped and whipped around in her seat. *Oh no! It's* him *again,* she realized, shock coursing through her body. *Just ignore him and he'll go away.*

Stu smiled up at her. Through the overcast sky the sun beat down with brutal intensity. But that did nothing to conceal the fact that Stu's upper body was lean and rippling with muscles under his ragged T-shirt. His tanned skin was almost caramel in color, a perfect contrast for his nearly white blond hair and very faded cutoff shorts.

"Stu," Nina croaked. *That's all I need, another dog on this beach,* she thought, irritated. *Stu and Mr. Green Shorts are probably old surfing buddies.*

"I wanted to see how you were feeling. You were pretty wiped out yesterday." He shaded his eyes as he peered up at her. "But you're looking good now."

Nina cleared her throat and said in her coolest voice, "I'm fine. Thanks for your concern."

"You don't have to thank me," Stu said softly.

Thoroughly annoyed, Nina kept her eyes fixed on the surf. "I never know what to say to you, Stu," she muttered.

"Sure, you do." Stu's tone was relaxed. "Just say what you think."

"If I were *Zen*-a, Warrior Princess, I might do that," Nina retorted. "But I'm into physical science, mind you, so I rely on my *brain*."

"The two are linked, you know."

A shrieking, giggling little boy raced in front of Stu, waving a large, jagged stick. Nina frowned. She had work to do, and Stu was deliberately distracting her. "Look, Stu, I'm not sure you noticed, but I guess your ESP is on the blink today. Anyway, I am *on duty*. That means I have to pay constant attention to the job at hand." Nina blew her whistle with all her might at the little boy, hoping Stu would get the hint.

Stu nodded agreeably. "Catch you later, little mermaid." He ambled off across the sand and sat down a few feet away. He slid on his sunglasses and looked totally relaxed.

Nina turned her eyes back to the beach. The little boy had handed over the stick, and everything was peaceful once again. But it didn't take long before the view became *much* more interesting. A stunning blond girl who filled out her shiny, gold bikini to perfection strolled over to Stu's side.

Nina strained to hear the exchange.

"Hi," the blonde said. "How's it going?"

"Can't complain," Stu answered.

The blonde beamed. Nina seethed. Cold anger sped through her veins, and she found herself gripping the arms of the lifeguard chair.

As he pulled up to the boardwalk surrounding Sweet Valley Shore, Winston turned on the calliope music. Just like before, kids flooded the street and surrounded his truck. He got out and yelled, "Hi, kids! Why don't you all line up and—"

"Hey, Bozo, who let you out of the circus?"

A stocky, curly-haired boy of about ten in a Batman T-shirt pushed his way to the front, a big sneer on his face. A few of the other kids started giggling.

Winston froze. Now what? *You're in charge, don't forget,* he reminded himself. *Rise above this, Egbert. Maybe the little brat will go away.* "OK, kids, line up," Winston ordered in what he hoped was a commanding voice. Apparently it was not.

Bat Boy laughed loudly. "Who's gonna make us? You and your phony mustache?"

Before Winston could stop him, the boy reached up and tugged on Winston's furry fake whiskers. "Yeow!" Winston howled. Half of his mustache hung free. The spirit glue and what felt like a good portion of Winston's skin had been pulled away with it.

"Ha, ha! Lookit!" his pint-size tormentor shouted. "Bozo is falling apart. He's a fake!"

"Hey, that's not funny," Winston panted as he tried reattaching the mustache. It refused to stick.

All the other kids started snickering and pointing at Winston's half-naked, half-mustached face. Their shrill voices rose to crescendo. As if on cue, a breeze suddenly sent his top hat tumbling off. Bat Boy snatched up the hat and put it on his own head.

"You'd better give me that," Winston ordered, his voice breaking embarrassingly on the word *give*. The world was blurring around him, and all he could see was what looked like an endless sea of laughing kids. *They're monsters, total monsters,* he thought in desperation.

"Na, na-na na na," the kid taunted, dancing just out of Winston's reach. "You're not Bozo, Bozo. You're *Squeaky!*"

"I *said*," Winston repeated, bearing down on the brat. *"Give me that hat."*

"Here it is," a familiar voice chirped sweetly.

Winston groaned out loud. Out of thin air Jessica Wakefield had appeared, his hat in her hand. She looked sharp and cool in her official lifeguard jacket and red swimsuit. She stood there grinning, her blue-green eyes bright with amusement.

Let me die right now, Winston thought, horrified, feeling his face flame. *Let the ground open up and swallow me.*

"What's the matter, Winnie?" Jessica asked. "Aren't you going to say thank you?"

"Thank you, Jessica," Winston said in an elaborately cheerful voice as he put the hat back on. He pulled the dangling mustache off his face and tried not to wince at the pain.

Bat Boy chanted, "We want free ice cream! We want free ice cream!" It soon caught on

137

with the rest of the maniacal crowd.

Winston looked at the sea of deceptively innocent little faces, their voices dripping with venom. *This is straight out of Stephen King,* he thought, recoiling.

Jessica raised a tanned, slim hand to smooth back wisps of her glossy hair. "Interesting career move," she said with a straight face. After a beat she burst into a fit of giggles.

"I know, I know," Winston muttered. "Believe me, I'm having second thoughts."

"I came up here to see what all the fuss was," Jessica said loudly over the din. "I *never* imagined that *you'd* be the cause of it."

"Look, um, I'm in kind of a sticky situation here." Winston paused, afraid to admit defeat. "Actually, Jess, I'm pretty desperate."

"Ice cream will do that to you. Or so I've heard."

Winston groaned loudly. He had no choice. He had to throw his manly pride by the wayside; it was time to beg. "*Please,* Jessica. Can you help me out somehow?"

Jessica nodded, still grinning. "Sure thing, Winnie." She turned and faced the shrieking crowd. She blew her whistle loudly. Instantly the children began covering their ears and wincing. They shrank away like baby vampires at the first sign of sunrise.

"OK, Mr. Freezee," she bellowed. "You're blocking traffic here! Now let's give him some room, kids. Out of the way."

Winston watched in awe as the brat pack instantly dispersed without a single wisecrack or argument.

"Wow, Jessica, I'm impressed. Thanks," he said weakly. "Just . . . just don't tell anyone you saw me, OK?"

"No problem," Jessica responded pleasantly. She looked Winston up and down and shrugged. "I've always had a weakness for a man in uniform."

Winston chuckled. "Thanks again, Jess." He climbed back into the truck and started the engine. "I really appreciate it."

"You owe me *big* time, Winnie," Jessica said, winking.

"I know, I know." Winston groaned as she waved him on.

"You look kind of lonely sitting there all by yourself," the blonde in the silvery suit purred, reaching out a finger to stroke Stu's shoulder.

What a line! Nina wanted to shriek out loud. She couldn't wait to see Stu give in.

"Mind if I join you?" The girl leaned forward, displaying her multitude of charms.

This is it, Nina thought, outraged. *Stu's about to*

show his true colors. Just watch him roll over and beg.

"Sorry," Stu said with an apologetic shrug. "But I'm kind of taken. This gorgeous mermaid floated into my life, and she's got me totally stoked." He gave the girl a mellow, friendly smile. "You know how it is."

The blond girl glared at him. "No, I *don't,* actually," she snapped before stomping off.

Mermaid! Nina's head reeled. *Gorgeous mermaid? Totally stoked?* She glanced over at Stu. *I thought for sure he'd be turning around to look at me or to wink "knowingly,"* she thought in surprise. *But he's not.*

Nina reached up and touched her face. It was burning hot. *After all the grief I gave him, he's actually . . . he's actually pledging to be faithful!* she realized. *How could all those crazy things I said come true in one man?*

Stunned, Nina picked up the water bottle from the tower floor and started misting her face like crazy. *Stu is the real thing—sensitive and caring.* Nina stole another glimpse of Stu, his lean, well-developed legs stretched out in front of him. *He's exactly like the dream man I described to Jessica—right down to the muscular calves. He even lives on a deserted island. Somehow my fantasy has come to life!*

Chapter Nine

"And I still don't know what it's all about. Imagine that!" Jessica complained, wrinkling her nose and slamming *Crime and Punishment* shut. She blinked hard as the wind blew a speck of sand in her eye. "All I know is that I have got to make Ben think I really understand this dumb book."

"Maybe it's not worth it," Miranda suggested. "You shouldn't knock yourself out."

"Maybe not." Jessica yawned. "I mean, watching paint dry would be more exciting than reading this."

"Then give yourself a break." Miranda picked up the binoculars and scanned the beach-scape. "Nothing. Your sister was right about Tower Three. She warned me that it might be a little slow around here today."

Why does my sister always focus on boring little work details instead of my romantic problems? Jessica wondered. *Elizabeth can be so insensitive sometimes.* She unfastened the tight red banana clip from her hair and threw it in her tote. When the wind blew her loose hair around her face, she immediately felt better.

"I guess you're right, Miranda. If I blew this, Ben and Priya would have a field day with me," Jessica said dramatically, reaching one hand up to massage her temples. "I'd never get Ben back then, for sure." *Though how Ben could prefer a snooty black-haired witch to me, I'll never understand,* she added silently.

Jessica stared out at the dunes and watched as the wind whipped up the sand. Some kid's inflated toy—a pink flamingo—bounced and rolled by. *Why should I give up now?* she wondered. *Me? Jessica Wakefield give up in her quest for the hottest guy around? That's totally not like me! Besides, how could I do all this work for nothing?*

"Ryan was right about the weather," Miranda commented. "The wind could cause some trouble today."

"Mm-hmm," Jessica hummed, distractedly flipping the book in her hands.

"Jessica, you're not actually thinking of—"

"Quiz me!" Jessica cried, tossing the book in Miranda's lap. "Go ahead."

"Oh no. You can't keep driving yourself—"

"Come on. Pleeese?" Jessica begged. "I just want to sort of, like, sharpen my skills. Just in case."

Miranda sighed. "You're a real trooper, Jess," she said, smiling. "OK. Summarize the story for me."

"Well, there's this main character, a guy named Ras . . ." Jessica brightened and snapped her fingers. "Raskolnikov! And he's this poor student. He talks about how people only care about material things."

"That's great!" Miranda patted Jessica's shoulder. "That's one of the keys to understanding the story."

"Let's see; there's more—" Jessica scrunched up her face painfully. "Jeez, this classical literature stuff is so hard to *understand*, let alone remember. It all begins with—"

"Uh-oh. Ix-nay on the usty-Day," Miranda hissed, handing the book back hastily.

"What?"

"Lose the book, Jess. Ben and Priya are coming over here, like *now!*"

"Oh no!" Jessica's heart leaped. Hands sweaty and trembling, she reached for her tote bag; it slid from her grasp and tumbled to the floor. Her eyes blurred as she scooped up the tote a second time and unzipped it. *Please, book.*

Please, please, please go in, she begged frantically. But it wouldn't fit, no matter how hard she tried. Breathing quickly, Jessica emptied the tote's entire contents onto the wood floor. Her hairbrush, sunscreen, lipstick, and lotion rolled and clattered at her feet.

Hurry, she told herself. *Get it in there.* But her fingers were clumsy and the book slid free. Jessica watched in horror as it spun slowly, gracefully through the air and landed in the sand—right at Priya's feet.

Priya knelt gracefully and scooped it up. "*What* do we have here?" she asked mockingly. She dusted off the sand and pretended to study the cover. "Why, it's a copy of *Crime and Punishment*! Isn't that amazing, Ben?" Priya held up the book for Ben to see. "Weren't we just talking about Dostoyevsky yesterday? What a surreal coincidence!"

Ben's face was blank, his eyes hidden by his sunglasses. "Wonders never cease."

Priya took off her sunglasses. Her dark eyes glittered with amusement. "Dostoyevsky, Jessica? I'm surprised—his name alone has four syllables. Way out of your league, I'd say."

Jessica fired a look at Ben; he stood in place, impassive. Jessica felt a surge of indignation. But she was mortified—too mortified to speak.

"Actually, Priya, Jessica was looking for a little

light reading," Miranda offered smoothly. "You know—some fun beach book. So I loaned her my copy of *Crime and Punishment*. She's already finished it, so I'll have to find her something else."

"Puh-leeze! Jessica probably finds *TV Guide* a challenge. Besides, this book just happens to look brand-new." She snorted and rolled her eyes. "Tell me another one, Miranda."

"Appearances are deceiving, Priya," Jessica snarled. "You shouldn't judge a book by its cover. I'd like it back, if you don't mind."

"No problem." She tossed the book up to Jessica and clapped mockingly when Jessica caught it. "At least you have good hand-eye co-ordination," Priya said with a snicker. "But then again, so does a monkey."

"Better a monkey than a conceited snake!" Jessica snapped.

Priya's face looked like a thundercloud. "You little—"

"Priya, we have to go," Ben cut in. "Ryan asked us to remind Miranda and Jessica about the red flags." Ben glanced up toward them. "Now they've been told, so let's go."

Priya's caramel complexion burned crimson. "What-*ever*. We *do* have better things to do." As Ben took her arm to lead her away, she paused. "And by the way, Jessica. I almost forgot. You'd

145

better study hard because there's going to be a quiz."

"He's gone," Nina murmured out loud as she cupped her hands over her eyes and scanned the beach.

"What did you say, Nina?" Theo asked absently, eyes glued to his binoculars.

"Uh . . . nothing," Nina lied, embarrassed that she'd spoken out loud. It wasn't that she actually cared one way or the other about where Stu was; she'd just been so busy with Theo that she hadn't even noticed Stu had left.

"I can't believe those parents," Theo remarked angrily. "They're just standing there. Sure, those kids aren't that young—I'd guess they're around ten or twelve years old—but still, whatever happened to common sense? Ryan only just took down the No Swimming signs, and now these kids are clinging to the raft like they can't swim to begin with."

It's just as well Stu left. I didn't need him hanging around all day, Nina told herself, half listening to her partner. Absently she brushed her hair back from her shoulders.

An older couple strolled by and paused to ask Nina how late the beach stayed open. Nina answered courteously and smiled politely, but she couldn't keep her mind off Stu. *No guy could be that wonderful,* she mused. *But I have to admit, he didn't let any of those beach bunnies lure him away.* Nina smiled absently and turned her attention back to the water. Suddenly the waves were jacking up and the sea seemed to boil over onto the beach. The water looked wild, dark, and menacing.

"I can't see the kids!" Theo cried. "All I see is the raft! They're in trouble!" He blew his whistle twice loudly as a warning to the other lifeguards before grabbing the red buoy and swinging it over his shoulder. Grim faced, Theo jumped the five feet down to the beach. He tore across the sand, his long brown legs a blur.

All thoughts of Stu evaporated. Nina's heart thumped like mad as she snatched up the orange buoy from her lap and sprang down from the tower. In seconds she was closing the gap behind Theo. Adrenaline poured through her body, but she forced herself to breathe steadily and not hyperventilate. Light-headedness and a shortage of oxygen to the lungs could be lethal for a lifeguard.

When the water nearly reached her knees, Nina flung herself in, plunging after Theo while she timed her movements with waves. As she hit deep water, swells crashed high above her, and her vision was momentarily obscured by solid sheets of gray water. Gasping, she made sure she caught air and breathed steadily so she wouldn't get too tired or weak.

"I've got one!" Theo shouted over the churning surf. He was holding on to a boy who looked about twelve. The boy's face was contorted with fear.

Nina knifed through the water, fighting the powerful currents. She frantically searched the waves until finally she spotted a blond head bobbing in the water. The tension in Nina's chest eased a fraction, and she slammed forward.

"Everything's going to be all right," Nina panted, trying to reassure the small, white-faced girl who was flailing wildly. She pushed the buoy toward the girl. "Hold on to this and I'll pull you in," she shouted, but the waves were crashing in all directions, making it harder to paddle and stay afloat. In less than a second the girl was carried off in the opposite direction. Just then a giant swell rose and knocked Nina back, but she fought and pushed ahead, every muscle screaming with agony. She strained against the powerful current until her fingers finally clasped the girl's thin wrist.

Nina shoved the buoy into her arms and turned toward shore. "You're safe now. You're doing great," she called out over her shoulder. Her last command was, "Hold on and don't let go!"

The girl looked too terrified to disobey. Luckily the kids hadn't floated out too far; if they had, it could have been a disaster.

Theo was right beside her, his dark curls just visible through the waves. Relief poured over Nina as they finally hit sand.

Gasping, Nina stumbled out of the water with the girl clambering right after her. The girl was coughing and choking but seemed for the most part to be all right. Nina checked her out and was relieved to see no signs of hypothermia, shock, or injury. The girl wasn't even throwing up seawater.

Theo carried the shivering boy and laid him gently on the wet sand. He too seemed to be in remarkably good shape. A small crowd of curious onlookers gathered a few feet away, but Nina was too absorbed to give them more than a passing glance.

"My baby!" the girl's mother wailed. She was sitting next to her daughter and weeping. The father angrily demanded to speak to someone in charge.

Nina stepped forward. "Sir, I'm a senior lifeguard," she began in her most soothing voice, though she was breathing hard from all the exertion. "Your children are safe and appear to be uninjured, but you may want to have them checked out. We can get the Jeep down here and have them transported to the local hospital if you want. . . ."

The father glared at her. "What *I* want to know is why you weren't watching them in the first place!"

Why weren't you? Nina thought sourly, but she kept her expression and tone even. "I understand that you're upset," she said gently. "You have every right to be shaken up."

"Well . . ." The father hemmed and hawed before turning to his wife. "Let's just take the kids to the doctor and put this behind us."

"We can't thank you enough," the mother added tearfully. "You both were wonderful."

"Yeah, uh, me too, I guess." The father glanced around with a small frown. "By the way, what happened to the raft?"

Nina pointed. Far out in the ocean, growing smaller and smaller, the orange raft drifted. The parents fell silent, perhaps realizing what a close call their children had had. As all four walked away the mother turned to call, "Thanks again for everything!"

"Man, am I relieved," Theo said, still breathing loudly as they walked back to the tower.

Nina nodded, adjusting the strap of her buoy. "You can say that again."

"The girl was really impressed with you," Theo teased, nudging Nina. "She told me she wanted to be a lifeguard just like 'the pretty lady.'"

Nina chuckled. "I don't mind a little hero worship, especially if it encourages her to learn how to swim. Her family too." She waved over to Ryan. He was only a few yards away, alert and ready to act if necessary.

"Everything OK?" Ryan asked.

"Fine," Theo replied. "They're taking the kids to get checked out just in case."

"Good job, guys," Ryan said as he strode over to join them. "You saved the kids and handled the parents." He gave Nina's shoulder a quick pat.

Nina smiled wearily and nodded.

"I'll head back with you and make out our report," Theo said to Ryan. "I'll be back, partner." He grinned at Nina before following Ryan across the sand.

"No problem," Nina mumbled as she stopped to catch her breath. Every muscle in Nina's body was suddenly aching. She felt as if she could curl up on the sand and fall right to sleep. *I feel like Gumby,* Nina thought, yawning. *Like I don't have a bone in my body.* It was typical of a rescue. First there was the big rush of adrenaline and stress, then the physical letdown.

As she walked to the tower Nina inhaled and exhaled until she felt steady. She climbed the ladder slowly, her legs trembling a little with fatigue. It would feel marvelous to sit down and massage her tired muscles.

When she reached her seat, she halted dead in her tracks. Someone had left something there.

Nina blinked and rubbed her eyes, wondering if she were seeing things. But it was still there—a big, beautiful conch shell holding down what looked like a note. The paper was encircled by colorful, polished stones from the sea. Unnerved, Nina grabbed the paper and read the message.

To my beautiful heroine. You really are a mermaid. —S.

Dazed, Nina collapsed into Theo's chair. She then picked up the shell and held it against her cheek.

Chapter
Ten

"Talk about walking into the lion's den," Elizabeth mumbled to herself as she let herself into the main lifeguard tower and headed for the door to Ryan's living quarters. She recalled only too clearly how Ryan had acted earlier— how distant and testy he had been. It had been a long, draining day; Elizabeth felt as if she'd run a twenty-four-hour marathon. But instead of a rest, all she had to look forward to was a heavy discussion with Ryan. Biting her lip, she knocked tentatively.

As she waited, Elizabeth gazed out the large glass windows in the Main Tower. The sun was starting to sink in the sky, and the wind was finally dying down. Elizabeth glanced down at the outfit she'd changed into after work: narrow white pants and a matching sleeveless top that flattered her smooth tan and golden hair.

Sighing, Elizabeth knocked again, more firmly this time. Silence. *He* knows *I'm coming over,* she thought in annoyance. *What could be taking him*— Suddenly the door flew open, interrupting her.

"Elizabeth, hi," Ryan said quietly, his honey-flecked eyes brushing over her face delicately before looking away. "Sorry—I wasn't sure I'd heard you at first. I was washing dishes, and the water was running." He reached underneath the left sleeve of his faded, baggy Surf Hawaii T-shirt, revealing a tanned, toned bicep while he scratched his shoulder.

Against her will Elizabeth's heartbeat began to race. She loved to see this more casual side of Ryan. While he never stopped being a vigilant, dedicated lifeguard—even in his sleep, she was sure—just seeing him hanging out in his sparsely furnished room dressed in old, worn, hanging-out clothes made him seem even more sweetly handsome and desirable than ever. She swallowed loudly, trying to overcome the flood of emotions washing over her. Elizabeth was here to have a serious talk; this was no time to turn to mush.

Was his running-water excuse for real? she wondered hastily. *I hope Ryan wasn't trying to avoid me.* Silently Elizabeth followed Ryan inside, noting the tense set of his shoulders. His small, efficient room looked just as tidy and clean as always.

"Come in and sit down," Ryan said with a weak smile that instantly crumbled. He waved his hand toward the tweed sofa. "Would you like a soda or something? If you're hungry, I could—" Elizabeth caught his hand and pulled him down to sit beside her. "Ryan," she said firmly, "no more stalling. We have to talk."

"I know," Ryan answered in a low voice, his eyes averted. "I—I just don't know where my mind's at lately. I guess I kind of lost it with those guys on the beach."

"You sure did—and you ended up taking it out on *me*. That's why I'm trying to understand what's going on, Ryan."

"I'm sorry. Really."

"Apology accepted, but you need to tell me everything." She paused. "Everything about Patti." He remained silent, so she prodded him. "Why didn't you tell me she was drinking again?"

He shrugged but still didn't speak.

"Ryan, please say something."

"This is so hard," Ryan muttered, looking down at his hands.

"Try, please," Elizabeth urged gently. "Just talk to me."

He shook his head.

"You can tell me anything."

"But you don't know what it's like!" Ryan blurted. "It's hard to explain to someone who hasn't gone through . . ." His voice trailed off, and he twisted his hands together violently.

"I know I don't have an alcohol problem, but I'm trying to understand," Elizabeth said, willing him to meet her eyes. She fumbled for the right words. "It must be rough to watch someone else fall off the wagon. Especially your sponsor. She was your role model, your source of inspiration. Now that's all going to waste."

"It's not just that," Ryan interjected, grimacing and running his hands through his hair. "Seeing Patti—it's made me think about . . . you know what I mean."

Elizabeth's eyebrows raised in response, and he winced as if he didn't want to explain. "It's . . . it's almost like Patti's backsliding is contagious."

"But *you* haven't had a drink, Ryan," Elizabeth said, her heart sinking when he didn't reply. "Have you?"

"If someone just breathes on me, I'll topple right over," Nina moaned. It had been a long day, a regular roller-coaster ride for her emotionally. "Making a save is always tiring, but I've never felt like *this* before. . . ."

Nina flopped back on her bed and stared at the pattern of paint on her ceiling. She shifted but couldn't get comfortable. Her face felt warm while the rest of her felt chilled. "Maybe I'm coming down with something," she murmured, pressing her hand to her forehead. It didn't feel all that feverish.

Breathing deeply, Nina closed her eyes. Almost immediately she felt a little dizzy. And weak. Visions of food hovered before her. Nina pulled the belt of her robe tighter and tried to push the images away. As soon as she had gotten home she'd grabbed a couple of apples for a quick snack and then had headed for the shower. But now the apples felt as if they were rattling around inside her stomach.

Images of lasagna and pizza still danced before Nina's eyes. That's what she needed—after her big save, she needed *sustenance.* Nina got up and padded downstairs to the kitchen. She pulled a can of vegetable soup from the cupboard and stared at it. *Stu's veggie soup was delicious—much better than anything out of a can,* she thought wistfully.

Nina slammed the can back into the cupboard loudly. "Getting sappy over soup?" she asked herself out loud. "Get a grip!"

Sighing, Nina opened the refrigerator and

cobbled together the ingredients for a ham sandwich; after all, *she* was no vegetarian. She fixed it and began to eat, but oddly the ham seemed dry, gritty, and tasteless. Her appetite vanished instantly, and she emptied the half-eaten sandwich into the trash. *Maybe going veggie isn't such a bad idea,* she thought. *Especially when everything tastes like sand.*

As she rinsed the dishes in the sink Nina became uncomfortably aware of how quiet the house was. Jessica was holed up in her room for some reason, and everyone else was out. Nina wished the pipes would rattle or something, but the eerie silence continued.

It's a good night to sit around and think, she told herself as she headed up to her room. *There are plenty of things I could think about. Things like surfboards and tattoos and seashells and* zanikus *and—*

"No! I just need *sleep*," Nina told herself. "Enough of these crazy thoughts. Everything will be normal again tomorrow."

"Please, Ryan, you know you can tell me anything," Elizabeth pleaded, her heart breaking at the thought of Ryan throwing away his sobriety. "You haven't backslid, have you?"

Ryan rubbed his eyes and shifted his position on the couch. "No, Liz. I—I've thought about it a few times, but I stopped myself." He turned to meet her gaze; his eyes were totally open, wide and trusting. Elizabeth knew he wasn't hiding anything from her anymore.

"Good." She reached over and took Ryan's hand. "You're not like Patti, Ryan. You're stronger."

"But I've *thought* about it," Ryan said, his voice straining with emotion. "That's just as bad as taking a drink."

"No, it's not!" Elizabeth insisted. "You haven't given in, Ryan. I know you won't."

"I just . . . sometimes . . . I don't know anymore, Liz—"

"But *I* do. You just have to take it one day at a time. And I'm here to help you get through it."

Ryan swallowed hard. As if his life depended on it, he turned to Elizabeth and kissed her. "Thank you, Liz," he said softly, turning away again. "That means a lot to me. But—"

"But what?"

"I'm still worried about Patti," Ryan admitted. "I wish I could help her."

"You can only offer your support, Ryan," she said, touching his shoulder. "Patti has to want to help herself. The only person you need to help right now is you." Elizabeth lightly stroked his cheek. "I don't understand why you didn't tell me about this in the first place. Why the secrecy?"

Sighing, Ryan pulled Elizabeth into his arms. She could feel the rapid beat of his heart. His body felt warm and strong against hers, and some of the tension inside her eased.

"I didn't want to spoil what we have between us," Ryan whispered, kissing her hair. "I knew you'd be upset by the news."

"So why did you bring me over to Patti's?" she asked gently as she slipped her arms around his waist.

"I was hoping Patti would pull herself together. I guess I thought she wouldn't drink in front of you. I was wrong." His voice grew husky. "But I'm not wrong about *this*." Ryan brushed his lips against hers and ran his fingers through her silky hair. "I love you, Elizabeth."

"I love you too, Ryan," she murmured before his lips met hers, this time more passionately. Elizabeth felt herself melt into Ryan's embrace, all her cares and worries disappearing with each passing second. Trembling, she clung to him, feeling the muscles in his back tighten and release with every kiss. The sensation made her dizzy. His mouth seemed hungry and demanding, and Elizabeth found herself pulling away, gasping for air.

"Ryan, listen to me." She put her hand on

his shoulder and leaned back. "From now on we have to be totally honest with each other. Promise?"

Ryan paused for a moment, a wistful smile growing imperceptibly on his face. "All right," he agreed tenderly, raining soft kisses on her forehead. "No more secrets."

For a long, peaceful moment they simply held each other. Elizabeth felt their hearts beating together in unison. Every few minutes Ryan would reach up and stroke her face or her hair; tingling with joy, she would wrap her arms around him more tightly and snuggle.

"Hey, Liz, I've got an idea," Ryan said, breaking the silence. "Why don't we get away from all this and go out to dinner tomorrow, just you and me? I know a great seafood restaurant in Berriston, about a half hour from here. It's the best-kept secret in southern California."

"Mmm," Elizabeth moaned dreamily. "My mouth is watering just thinking of it."

"You know, this time of year is really important to me," he said, his tone deeply serious. "It means I've made it through another year. . . ." His eyes turned pleading, vulnerable.

Of sobriety, Elizabeth finished silently as she put her finger to Ryan's lips. She nodded to show him she knew what he meant.

"It would mean so much to me, Liz. We . . . we

have a lot we need to celebrate." He kissed her on the corners of her mouth. "And a lot to be thankful for."

"I know, Ryan," Elizabeth said warmly, pride shining in her eyes. "I wouldn't miss it for the world."

Jessica hurled *Crime and Punishment* with all the force she could muster. It made a dull thud and slid clumsily to the floor.

"That didn't feel half as good as I thought it would," she grumbled, picking up the book. "Maybe I should throw something breakable— something that would make a nice big crash."

Jessica searched the room for something appropriate and blinked in disbelief when her gaze fell on the clock radio. She'd been reading for nearly three hours. *I've totally lost track of time,* Jessica realized, amazed. *I've never studied this long without a break. Well, it might as well have been a hundred hours. I still don't understand what this book is about.*

Voices drifted up from downstairs, and Jessica's stomach clenched. One voice was deep and sexy, the other phony and high-pitched. *Priya and Ben!* They were downstairs talking—and they *had* to know she was upstairs!

"Well, I'm not going to fall into Priya's

web," she whispered to herself, gripping the book. "I'm staying out of sight."

Jessica carefully inched toward her door and quietly opened it. She pressed her ear to the crack and listened. It wasn't hard to hear them; they were incredibly loud.

"The grilled swordfish was so delicious tonight, Ben," Priya cooed. "But the conversation was even better."

Jessica heard Ben laugh softly, and her chest tightened in response. "You're only saying that because it's true," Ben teased. "I have to admit, you're never at a loss for words."

"You know, every other man I've dated thought I was too much of a challenge," Priya replied. "I guess I intimidated them."

Jeez, how modest can you get? Jessica wondered, making a face.

"Well, it's not surprising," Ben said calmly. "You're both gorgeous *and* brilliant. I happen to like a woman with substance. Beauty can only go so far."

Jessica glared in front of her as the conversation took an uncomfortable, giggly pause. Rising anger made it hard for her to sit quietly. Her fingers curled reflexively around the book as if it were possible to strangle it. Not wanting to hear any more, she shut the door quietly.

I'll show them, she thought as she tiptoed

back to her bed. Jessica had begun to slam *Crime and Punishment* down on it repeatedly when she suddenly became aware of something very distressing.

She had to use the bathroom.

Jessica groaned and sat down on the bed. How could she leave her room without them finding out? The floors in the old house were awfully creaky. If they caught her, she'd be doomed for sure.

Jessica stood up and lightly hopped in place. Maybe if she kept moving, the urge would go away. *Try to put it out of your mind,* she told herself, but it was no good; in a matter of seconds her condition had become worse. She tried wringing *Crime and Punishment* viciously in her hands, but that didn't work either. Grimacing, she let the book drop to the bed.

I can't wait anymore, Jessica realized. *I'll have to chance it. Maybe if I'm really, really quiet, I can slip past them.* Noiselessly as possible, she opened the door a tiny crack and slipped through. *Maybe they'll be too busy discussing their mutual brilliance to notice,* she hoped, her heart racing.

Jessica gulped and slid stealthily along the wall, one step at a time, every tiny squeak making her pulse zoom faster. She tugged at the bottom of her white sleep tee. *I wish I was wearing black,* she mused. *Then I'd blend in the shadows better.*

But just as she began passing the stairs she got a double whammy; she not only stepped on a loudly groaning board but also caught a huge splinter in the ball of her foot.

"Yeeouch!" she squealed, clapping her hand over her mouth.

"Is that you, Jessica?" Ben called.

Gasping in surprise, Jessica spun around to make a run for it, but she slipped. She stumbled and felt everything around her lurch. She was about to fall down the stairs—backward!

Nina just couldn't sleep. Every time she'd be just about to drift off, she'd hear some creak in the wood or Jessica banging around, and she'd be wide awake again.

Come on, Nina, let's face it, the noises aren't what's keeping you awake, a voice inside her head told her. *It's—*

"No, it's not," Nina assured herself, taking calm, measured breaths to slow down the beating of her heart. "That's not it at all."

She turned onto her other side and listened to the sounds of the ocean pouring in gently through her open window. It was so soothing, relaxing. All she had to do was let herself go with the flow of the sea and let the waves carry her away. Farther . . . farther . . . *farther* . . .

Nina bolted upright and shook her head vigorously. "I've got to do something about this," she mumbled, jumping out of bed and turning on the light. She grabbed the conch shell, sea stones, and note and wrapped them up in a towel. Her pulse pounding in her ears, she shoved the whole mess in the bottom drawer of her dresser, slammed it shut, and flipped off the light. *There*, she thought, getting back under the covers. *That ought to do it.*

Nina closed her eyes and let herself drift off again. She let herself dive fully into the ocean and swim through the waves toward . . . something. A large wooden object floated out on the water, calling to her. She strained to hear what it was saying, but she was too far away.

She pressed harder. Every stroke should have been sapping her energy, but for some reason the closer she got, the stronger she felt. Nina opened her eyes to see that she was swimming toward her own dresser. The bottom drawer opened and closed like a mouth as it said, "You really are a mermaid."

Gasping, Nina awoke from her dream. "This can't be happening," she breathed as she got up and turned on the light again. Defiantly she pulled the towel-wrapped bundle out of the dresser and carried it over to the closet. Nina took out one of her duffel bags, stuffed the bundle inside, zipped it up, and put it back in the closet. "Don't you dare come back out," she declared as she slammed the closet door shut.

Back in bed, Nina blinked but couldn't close her eyes. It was as if the note, the shell, and the stones were all calling out from their new hiding place like Edgar Allen Poe's Tell-Tale Heart. *We're here,* they seemed to say. *Don't ignore us.*

Nina turned her back toward the closet and put her pillow over her head. *Tomorrow morning you're gone,* she vowed. *Out the door. In the garbage. And out of my mind.* Yawning, Nina buried her face in the pillow. *Yeah, that's it. I'll take care of everything . . . tomorrow.*

Letting out a strangled cry, Jessica grabbed the railing and caught herself before she could fall, but the momentum forced her to scramble all the way down both stairwells; if she'd tried to stop, she'd have tripped over her own feet and broken her neck.

Maybe I should have taken that option, Jessica realized when she landed like a cat at the bottom of the stairs right in front of Ben and Priya, who sat snuggled together on the couch.

"Oops," Priya said with a big, fake smile. "We didn't mean to startle you."

Jessica gaped at the two of them, speechless.

167

She was still reeling from her near death experience.

"Is something the matter?" Priya cooed, cuddling up closer to Ben. "Why don't you sit down and tell us all about it."

As if I have a choice, Jessica realized. She needed to sit down and recover. Trying to look as cool and indifferent as possible, Jessica walked over and sat in the chair across from the sofa. Her legs were wobbly, and she prayed neither of them could see her trembling.

Smiling evilly, Priya watched her like a hungry cat would watch a trapped mouse. Ben sat glued to Priya's side, unsmiling and alert. All in all, Jessica felt as if she were in front of a firing squad.

"I'm dying to know what you thought of *Crime and Punishment,* Jessica," Priya began. Her voice sounded like the sharpening of knives. "Wasn't the landlady a perfect symbol of oppressive materialism?"

Jessica's blood turned to ice. When she caught Ben watching her with a curious, guarded expression, the icy blood rushed to her head, making it feel like it might shatter. *I've got to fake it somehow. I've done it before, and I'd better be able to do it now.*

With a toss of her hair, Jessica gave Priya a confident smile. "Well, that was obvious. So what?"

"I guess it was. But you have to admit that figuring out *why* Raskolnikov killed his landlady wasn't that easy."

Jessica shrugged and dug her fingers into the arms of the chair. "Maybe it wasn't to *you*."

"Who would have guessed he killed her because of the missing clock?" Priya ran her long, red nails through her hair. "What a surprise!"

Jessica smirked, feeling some of her strength returning. "A surprise? Hardly, Priya," Jessica boasted, deciding to bluff. "I figured that out right away." *Not that I remember any clock in the story,* Jessica thought.

"The landlady was going to sell the clock, of course. It was worth a lot of money. That's why Raskolnikov was so upset when it was missing," Priya said, nodding wisely.

"Sure, he was," Jessica ad-libbed. "The clock was worth about a million dollars."

Priya's eyes widened. "How impressive, Jessica. I'm amazed you remembered that. And how soon did you realize that Svidrigailov was in on the plot?"

"I knew *that* by the first chapter!" Jessica said haughtily. *All right!* she cheered silently. *I'm passing with flying colors.*

Suddenly Priya began laughing and rocking in her seat. "By the first chapter!" she repeated. "How *rich!*"

Jessica stared in confusion. A twinge of fear shot up her spine. "What's so funny?" she asked defensively, but Priya kept cackling.

"OK, OK." Ben finally spoke, his face beet red but blank. "That's enough. Game over."

"Game? What do you mean?" Jessica asked indignantly.

Ben's blue eyes met Jessica's for an unsettling moment. "Priya was pulling your leg, Jess. In the book it's never made clear exactly why Raskolnikov killed his landlady. And there was never any stolen clock."

"No stolen clock," Jessica echoed, feeling her stomach heave. Her mouth suddenly tasted sour—as sour as Ben's expression.

Ben shook his head. "And Svidrigailov had nothing to do with it. He wasn't in on any plot."

An enormous lump formed in Jessica's throat and her eyes felt hot. She swallowed hard. *I won't cry in front of this witch,* she vowed. "So you were just trying to make a fool of me."

Priya smiled viciously. "You did that all by yourself, Jessica." Priya slipped her hand through Ben's arm. "Let's get out of here, sweetie. There's got to be someplace where we can find *honest,* intelligent conversation." She rose and pulled Ben behind her. "We're certainly not going to get it here."

Silently Ben followed Priya across the living room and out through the door. Ben looked back at her once just as hot tears began to fill her eyes, but he turned away quickly. The door slammed, reverberating like a death sentence.

"I hate her," Jessica muttered, dashing away a stray tear with the back of her hand. How could Ben just sit there and let Priya demolish her? Even if he was no longer her boyfriend, he could have at least said *something* to get Priya to stop.

"I hate them both!" she screamed, tears streaming down her face. She tore upstairs, grabbed *Crime and Punishment* from her bed, and flew into the bathroom. Choking back a wail, she flipped open the toilet lid and for a long moment stared at the book, her body weakening under the weight of the humiliation it had brought her.

Angrily Jessica tore a section of pages and ripped them to shreds. Racked with sobs, she tossed the pieces into the bowl, flushed, and watched through her tears as the shreds gurgled down the pipes. She kept ripping and flushing until there was nothing left to do but cry.

Chapter Eleven

"This is hopeless," Nina grumbled. She closed her eyes tightly, but it wouldn't stop. The Sunday morning sunshine streamed relentlessly through her window. *I give up,* Nina thought in disgust. *I may not be ready to face the day, but it's here. And there's nothing I can do about it.*

Outside, birds were singing and chirping nonstop, making Nina want to scream. She clamped her hands over her ears. *Shut up, please!* she begged silently. Between the glaring sunshine and the birds, she was about to lose it. *Jeez. My nerves must be really fried if the twittering of birds is driving me over the edge.*

Nina rubbed her eyes and forced herself out of bed. She not only felt bone weary from yesterday's rescue but also very edgy. Things had kept waking her up all night—Jessica, Ben, and

Priya talking downstairs, the wind blowing against the shutters, the incessant flushing of the toilet at one point, and the whirling of her own mind.

Nina dragged herself over to the mirror above her dresser. She frowned at her reflection, complete with baggy eyes and puffy face. "Yuck," she said out loud, sticking out her tongue at herself.

I can't face the idea of dealing with people today. What I need is a hot shower—like right now! Nina slipped on her robe and took out her towel. She trudged to the bathroom, her feet dragging. *More important, I desperately need some time to unwind and relax,* Nina realized. She was supposed to be on duty in just over an hour, but feeling the way she did, she knew she'd be of no use.

The jets of steaming hot water felt good and eased some of the tension inside her. As she slathered on bath gel Nina came to a decision. She deserved a break today.

Swathed in a robe and towels, she walked back into her room. While she smoothed on some moisturizer, her gaze landed on her ten-speed, which was leaning against the wall. That was it! She'd go on a nice long ride, away from everyone and everything.

This will be a mental health day, Nina

173

explained to herself. *Elizabeth will cover for me. She'll understand.*

Nina threw on a pair of jeans and a tank top, slipped on her Keds, and quietly carried her bike down the stairs. She had already started to feel a little better. Eager to get outside, she parked the bike in the foyer and hurried into the kitchen. She scratched out a note to Elizabeth and propped it up on the table with the saltshaker.

Once she'd gotten outside and begun pedaling her way along the frontage road, the rising sun had spread a glorious wash of pinks, oranges, and yellows across the pale sky. Nina's smile widened as she pedaled quickly along the road, eager to make her escape. In minutes the beach house was far behind her.

Time passed quickly; the sun arced higher in the sky, and it was getting hotter. Nina was starting to perspire and breathe hard. She checked the speedometer; she'd barely gone over a mile, but she needed a breather.

The perfect resting spot lay a few feet away. A giant bristlecone pine tree spread its massive branches over a grass slope on the side of the road. It looked shady and cool underneath. Nina dismounted her bike and walked it over, hearing the strange word *tathata* echoing in her mind.

She sighed deeply and leaned against the ancient

bristlecone. It seemed familiar, as if it were an old friend, and its shade left her feeling refreshed and renewed. Reaching out a hand, she caressed the tree's rough bark. Her hand tingled, and a current of warmth seemed to travel through her. She felt more alive and aware, as if each nerve ending were galvanized.

Nina gazed around her; everything appeared brighter and clearer. The grass was greener, the sky bluer, the sun more golden. *I've never taken time to enjoy nature,* Nina thought hazily. *I've never really appreciated it.* She stroked the thick, gnarled roots radiating from the tree trunk. *This old tree is so masterful, so wise,* she mused, *yet so beautiful and gentle too. One could almost believe it has the power to heal. . . .*

"Why today, of all days, does Nina have to pull this?" Elizabeth groaned, slumping down in the kitchen chair. She pulled her terry cloth robe tighter while she reread the note, hoping against hope that it was all a mistake.

"What? What did she do?" Jessica mumbled, stirring her cup of coffee. She was already in her red lifeguard suit and wearing her sunglasses.

"She asked me to cover for her today."

"So? What's the problem, Liz? She'll owe you."

Elizabeth gulped down her orange juice.

"I'm going out with Ryan tonight and wanted to get my hair done first," she said, her tone rising. "I wanted to pick out a little gift for him too. Now what am I going to do? I'll barely have time to get *dressed*."

"Let someone else take Nina's shift, then," Jessica suggested, pushing away her empty cereal bowl.

"Ryan's already shorthanded without Nina. I can't leave him in the lurch like that."

"You're too conscientious," Jessica declared. "You're not responsible for *everything*, you know."

"I know," Elizabeth muttered. "But I can't help it." She gazed around the kitchen. Dishes were stacked in the sink, and crumbs covered the counter. "I guess everyone's left already but us," she said, not wanting to mention Ben by name.

Jessica just shrugged and pushed up her sunglasses. "Well, if you insist on doing double time, then maybe you should meet Ryan at the restaurant. That way you can run all your errands, and he'll be none the wiser."

Elizabeth rubbed her forehead and nodded. "You know, that's a good idea. I'll suggest that to Ryan this morning. Now, if you give me two minutes, I'll be dressed and ready." Elizabeth bolted up to her room, pulled on her suit, and brushed her hair back into a sleek ponytail. She snatched up her tote and slid her lifeguard whistle over her head last, as always. Then she rushed back down the stairs.

The sun was shining and puffy clouds raced across the sky as the twins cut across the dunes. Elizabeth could smell the fresh sea air and hear the rhythmic fall and rise of surf as they made their way over the sand.

Elizabeth glanced at her sister, who seemed as lost in thought as Elizabeth was. When Jessica took off her sunglasses to rub the bridge of her nose, Elizabeth could see how puffy her eyes were.

"Oh, Jessica," she gasped. "What's wrong? Have you been crying?"

Slipping her sunglasses back on, Jessica sniffled. "I had this incredible plan to win Ben back . . . ," she began, her voice breaking a little. "But it didn't exactly work."

Elizabeth raised her eyebrows questioningly.

"Priya was bragging about how she read this author Dusty . . . Dostoo . . ."

"Dostoyevsky?"

"Right. So I decided to read him too. I bought a copy of *Crime and Punishment* and everything. Well, she and Ben found out. . . ." Jessica's lower lip trembled.

"And? What went wrong?" Elizabeth prodded

gently. *I almost don't want to know,* she thought.

"Priya had a great time tearing me apart. She set me up and asked me all these trick questions to make me look stupid in front of Ben," Jessica mumbled, kicking up a cloud of sand. "And Ben just stood there and let her do it!"

Her heart aching for her sister, Elizabeth heaved a deep sigh. "Listen, Jess," she said after a second. "If Ben doesn't like you for yourself, then he's not worth it. As for Priya, just ignore her."

"I don't think I can do that, Liz," Jessica replied. "She really went over the line. I don't know what I'm going to do, but it's not over . . . not yet."

"Elizabeth! Jessica!" Ryan called from the Main Tower.

Jessica shrugged. "I guess duty calls," she said as they looked over and saw that the rest of the group was already gathered for work. "Thanks for listening."

Elizabeth hugged her twin tightly. "Just forget about it, Jessica. You're better than they are. Don't lower yourself to their level."

"OK. I won't." A smile spread across Jessica's face. "Race you!"

The twins bolted across the sand.

I'm lost, Nina thought as she pedaled along. *Who cares?*

The breeze blew through Nina's hair and she grinned, enjoying the feeling. Her strong legs pumped steadily as she steered her bike down yet another strange road. The air was cool, and the scent of the sea grew stronger and stronger. Soon the road curved right near the water.

Nina paused for a second, one foot resting on the ground, the other balancing on the pedal. *The ocean is so beautiful and alive,* she thought. Something silver flashed by, then disappeared. Her heart beat a little quicker.

Was that a dolphin? she wondered, straining to look across the azure, shimmering water. *Maybe it will resurface.*

She began riding again and a small bridge materialized before her. The sun beat down and turned everything into a pale, golden haze. Nina squinted as she pedaled across the bridge to the small island lying just on the other side.

A puffy cloud crossed in front of the sun, dampening its rays enough to bring into focus the enormous white adobe beach house that dominated the island. Coconut and palm trees swayed and dipped in the gentle breeze. Colorful wildflowers covered the front yard and spilled over onto the long, winding driveway. Seagulls swooped and squawked overhead, and the waves gently foamed up on the beach.

When she reached the end of the long,

winding driveway, Nina got off her bike and rolled it up to the house. When she passed by the silver VW Bug, a tingle shot up her spine.

The last time I was here, I was too sick to notice how beautiful and peaceful this place is, Nina thought dreamily. *It's like paradise. I wouldn't mind hiding out here.*

Nina leaned the bike against a palm tree and made her way to the front of the house as if she were being pulled by a magnet. She had just reached out a slim finger to ring the bell when the door automatically swung open in front of her.

He stood on the other side of the door, a glowing smile of approval on his face. He was wearing faded cutoffs like before, and his tanned, sculpted upper body was bare. His clear blue eyes glowed with emotion as he held out his hand.

"What took you so long?" Stu asked huskily, reaching out and carefully tracing Nina's face with his fingertips.

When Stu brought his lips to meet hers, Nina melted into his arms. Stu's kisses were warm and deep, with a ferocity that took her breath away. He smelled like soap, coconut oil, and the sun. His bare skin was smooth as silk beneath her hands. Nina could feel the savage beating of his heart against her chest as she held on to him as if for dear life.

Suddenly Stu lifted Nina into his arms and carried her to the couch, where they fell against the soft cushions. They clutched each other, their lips hungry, neither saying a word.

"OK, guys, let's get cracking," Ryan announced. "Everyone knows their assignments, so let's move." The group immediately dispersed and Ryan started toward the Main Tower.

Elizabeth hurried to his side. "Uh, Ryan, I'm covering for Nina this afternoon."

Ryan spun around, his expression darkening ominously. "You're kidding, I hope," he said sharply.

"Don't worry, I'll have plenty of time to get ready for our dinner date," she said quickly.

Ryan's jaw was tense, his broad shoulders stiff. She was anxious about continuing, but she had no choice. "Listen . . . I have a few errands to run beforehand, so why don't I just meet you at the restaurant?" Elizabeth offered. "That way I won't have to worry about getting back to the beach house in time for you to pick me up."

Ryan's expression softened a little. "Fine. That should work." He nodded confidently. "The reservations are for seven at the Captain's Feast in Berriston. Don't forget."

Elizabeth felt her heart melting. She leaned closer to him, and he bent down so she could kiss his ear. "I won't forget," she murmured. "You can count on me."

"They're making total fools of themselves," Jessica commented, her face crinkling in disgust as she bent to rub a little tanning lotion onto her sun-warmed legs. Even though it was a beautiful, picture-perfect Sunday, she couldn't enjoy it. "I mean, Ben and Priya are supposed to be patrolling for alcohol and dogs, not fooling around and putting on a show for everybody."

"If Ryan sees Priya goofing off, she'll be patrolling for a new job," Miranda remarked. "You know, I'm glad we got Tower Two today, Jessica. Look at all those gorgeous hunks playing beach volleyball right under our noses! This is quite a coup."

"Well, it's awfully hard for the guys to concentrate when half of them are watching Priya and Ben lock lips," Jessica muttered. When Priya pulled away and started mock posing for Ben in her suit, she gagged.

"What, does she think *Sports Illustrated* is going to just wander by?" Miranda quipped. "Or *Wild Kingdom*, maybe." She scratched her arm and frowned. "Darn, I'm peeling. Priya's always 'borrowing' my sunscreen, but *her* tan stays perfect."

"That's funny. I thought snakes shed their skin."

Miranda chuckled, and Jessica had started to join in when a loud cry captured her attention. In unison she and Miranda leaped to their feet.

"Something's wrong out near the jetty!" Jessica gasped as she peered into her binoculars. "Some people might be caught in a rip current!" Even though the ocean looked fairly peaceful, Jessica knew that was when it was most dangerous. Its appearance was deceptive, causing people to go out farther than they should.

"I'm on my way." Jessica caught up the buoy and sprang down from the tower, landing neatly in the sand. *My first save of the season,* she thought excitedly as the adrenaline raced through her body.

As Jessica sprinted along the beach in the direction of the far-off jetty, she heard Miranda calling behind her that she was getting the paddleboard. The scene blurred around her as she tore across the sand. She heard Miranda blow the whistle twice—a warning to the other lifeguards.

Jessica's heart hammered in her chest. Rip currents could be deadly, and bringing someone in from one was extra difficult. The only way to escape the lethal currents was to swim parallel to the beach until freed from the water's pull. Only then would Jessica and the person she'd be towing in be able to head for shore. *I can do it*, she told herself, her eyes scouring the waves for signs of the three swimmers as she pounded forward.

Suddenly something snagged Jessica's ankle and sent her sprawling headfirst into the sand. The buoy flew out of her hands. Jessica crashed hard, and the wind was knocked out of her.

Gasping and coughing, she lay stunned for a moment before trying to scramble to her feet. A shadow breezed past. Looking up, Jessica saw a flash of dark hair and an arm swooping up the buoy she had dropped. *Priya!*

"Hey!" Jessica shrieked.

"C'mon!" Priya shouted to Ben. Before Jessica could react, Priya had dashed into the water with Ben right beside her.

"Priya! You *witch!*" Jessica screamed, but the two were oblivious as they dove into the swells.

"No, no, *no!* I can't *believe* this!" Jessica rubbed her ankle and moaned. She couldn't stop herself from fuming, even though she knew it was useless. By now she could barely make out the two small specks that were Priya's and Ben's heads.

Holding back tears, Jessica got up on her knees and pounded her fist into the wet sand. "That was my save. *My* save!"

Chapter
Twelve

"Jessica! What happened?" Miranda asked urgently, a paddleboard under her arm.

Tears threatened to spill from Jessica's eyes. "Priya tripped me so she could steal my save!" She pointed at the jetty and then rubbed her sore ankle. There were three swimmers in the water, but only two lifeguards. "Go help them, Miranda. I think I'm hurt."

Miranda nodded and sped toward the water; in seconds she was knifing through the waves after Ben and Priya. Jessica watched, feeling helpless as tears of rage streamed down her face.

"What's going on here!" Ryan yelled, running up beside Jessica. He was breathing quickly, his buoy draped over his shoulder; she knew he was ready to back up the trio in the water. "Pull yourself together. This is no time to throw a tantrum!"

"But it's not my fault!"

Ryan trained his binoculars on the water and frowned. "What is your problem, Wakefield?" he growled. "Don't you realize there are lives at stake?"

Her blond ponytail bobbing, Elizabeth jogged over, her face twisted in concern. "Are you OK?" she asked.

Jessica wobbled to her feet and tested her ankle; it seemed to be uninjured. "Well, luckily I'm not hurt," she said petulantly. "But Priya tripped me, Ryan. Deliberately! She wanted to steal my save."

"There's no such thing as 'my' save or 'your' save, Jessica. We're all working together," Ryan replied. "And that's exactly why this situation worries me. Are you sure Priya tripped you?"

"I'm telling the truth." Jessica tossed her head, her eyes flashing. She dashed away angry tears with the back of her hand.

"I believe my sister, Ryan." Elizabeth's tone was firm.

Ryan ran one hand through his hair in apparent exasperation. "Look, we can talk about this later. Right now I need to keep an eye on this save." He stared into his binoculars. "So far, so good," he breathed.

"Thanks for your support, Ryan," Jessica said sharply. She glanced at Elizabeth for backup, but her twin gave a slight shake of her head instead.

"Go home, Jessica," Ryan ordered, "and cool off."

Jessica gritted her teeth. *Maybe Ryan will eventually realize what a horrible lifeguard Priya is, but I shouldn't push him,* she told herself. *I'm sure he knows that already.*

"Oh no!" Ryan cried out. "It looks like one of the swimmers is caught under the rocks." He dropped the binoculars to the sand and raced toward the ocean, his buoy flying behind him.

Jessica and Elizabeth both froze, their faces white. *If the swimmer's caught, he could easily die,* Jessica thought in horror, not wanting to say the words out loud. The jetty could be a killer at times.

"They can't pull him free," Elizabeth moaned after grabbing Ryan's binoculars to see for herself. "Ben and Priya are both diving now. Miranda's got the second swimmer, and . . ." Elizabeth grimaced. "It looks like the third guy's holding on to a buoy. Here comes Ryan!" She tensed as if ready to plunge in the water too.

Jessica's breath quickened. Her ankle ached mildly. *If only I could be out there,* she seethed. *There wouldn't have been any trouble if it was me making the save.*

187

Elizabeth suddenly exhaled loudly. "Ben just brought up the guy from under the rocks. He looks OK, but it's hard to tell from here. Wait . . . yes! They're bringing everyone in!" She was practically jumping and up down. "Ben looks relieved, so the guy must be fine."

Jessica spun on her heel and strode rapidly back toward the tower, struggling not to break down. *No way am I going to hang around and wait for Priya to get back. Watching her show off and act like some big hero would make me totally sick.*

She gritted her teeth and stomped across the sand. *I wasn't imagining things,* she thought fiercely. *Even Ryan will have to see the truth. Priya is threatened by me—so threatened by me, she'll stoop to sabotage!*

"I can survive this," Winston muttered as sweat dripped down his forehead. He'd been on his ice cream route for only two hours, but it felt more like two days.

He tugged at the front of his jacket, which now had a huge chocolate ice cream stain on it; his sleeves were decorated with blotches of strawberry and blueberry Popsicle drippings. One lone blob of vanilla ice cream marked the knee of his pants. He knew that Ms. Limgudder would freak out when she saw the uniform.

"Maybe she'll think I'm a work of modern art instead," he muttered.

The decibel level of the shrieking kids surrounding him rose, and Winston flinched. His eardrums were aching. *Kids today have no manners whatsoever,* he thought. *Yessiree, things were different in my day.*

Putting on a plastic smile, Winston reached inside the big freezer and pulled out a paper-wrapped, chocolate-dipped, chocolate chip cone. "OK, kids, who ordered the Double Choco Delite?" With his free hand Winston pushed back his top hat and cleared the little freeze-dried mustache hairs from his upper lip in one smooth movement.

A little red-haired girl reached for the cone. Her pink-flowered outfit made her look especially sweet, but Winston knew better than to trust appearances at this point.

Sure enough, the girl stared down at her cone before glowering back up at him. "This doesn't look like the picture." She pouted, pointing to the colorful illustrations of the desserts that had been painted on the truck's side panel. "It's a lot smaller."

A little girl with glasses piped up, "Don't pay for it, Amber. This guy's a rip-off."

"Rip-off, rip-off," the chant began.

Winston glanced around him. He was severely

outnumbered. "OK, kids," he shouted over the din, doing his best to look authoritative. "Let's all be quiet, or I can't take your orders."

The chanting grew louder, drowning him out, while Mean Red grinned venomously and began taking huge bites from her cone.

"Hey, you haven't paid for that yet," Winston scolded. "You bite it, you've bought it."

Ice cream dripped like poisonous slime down the front of the little girl's pink shirt. "Melissa's right. You're a cheater," she said defiantly. There was a rising murmur from the crowd, which stirred restlessly and seemed to be creeping closer. And closer. And closer.

Winston gritted his teeth. *Calm down. Breathe deeply.* He stood up straight and tried to look tough. *Whatever you do, don't show fear. These little kids are like sharks—they get mean if they smell blood.*

"Hey, mister!" a freckle-faced boy shouted, waving an empty Popsicle stick. "My Frostee Berry-Bear tasted like a dirty old sock! I want my money back."

"Yeah." Another boy with a crew cut stepped forward. "Mine's melting. I want a refund!" He shoved his Freezee Choco-Bot in Winston's face. The robot-shaped ice cream bar transformed into a vile and menacing blob before his very eyes.

Winston felt a hot tide surge up inside him. He was sweating bullets, but his hands felt icy—like two big Pinky-Linky Bunny Pops. Kids closed in on him, waving Double-Dippies, Razzie-Tazzies, and Jumbo Juicies in the air.

Suddenly he remembered something he'd learned long ago in first aid. He took a deep breath and felt the oxygen rush to his brain. "Stop!" he bellowed. "Now hear this. There will be no exchanges, no returns, and absolutely *no refunds!*"

There was a moment of utter silence. *I've stunned them,* Winston thought gleefully, his heart thumping. *It just goes to show you that we adults have to be firm. We have to be strong. It's the only thing these kids today understand. It's—*

"What's going on here!" A tall woman, who looked as large and muscular as a professional wrestler, came striding over in a hot pink work-out outfit. "My little Bambi says you're not giving the children what they want!" She cracked her knuckles, then gently took the hand of a small dark-haired girl with chocolate smeared all over her face.

"Uh . . . um . . . ," Winston stammered. "Well, you see—now, just a minute, lady. You have no idea what I've gone through today." *I'm the victim here,* he wailed to himself. *I'm the poor, maligned ice cream man. But does anyone worry about me? Noooo!*

191

"I really don't care," she shot back. "You'd better make these kids happy." She tapped her foot. "Or else."

Winston flinched; his number was up. But he had no idea how he could escape the minimob—or the towering, angry mother—unscathed. *What would James Bond do in this situation?* he wondered. *No, wait, never mind . . .* Suddenly an image flashed through his brain. Who had just recently saved him from a similar predicament? *Someone a lot tougher and cooler than 007,* he remembered, feeling a ray of hope. *Jessica Wakefield. I know what to do. . . .*

"I'm getting really hot," Nina said dreamily, leaning against Stu's shoulder. "I mean, the *fire's* getting really hot," she corrected, her cheeks burning. She and Stu were curled up on a big blanket on the sand in front of a crackling bonfire, the ocean roaring in the background. A delicate breeze caressed Nina's skin. She sniffed the crisp scent of the sea air and smiled.

"I can throw some water on the fire, I guess," Stu offered, pausing to kiss the top of Nina's head. He didn't appear to catch Nina's slip of the tongue. "I like the flames, though. They're so powerful and harmonious. All that color and heat—it's totally awesome."

Nina nodded, narrowing her brown eyes as

she studied the bright orange flames. "Let's not put it out. Let's just lie here and enjoy it." Nina sighed softly and cuddled closer to Stu. She traced the tattoo on his strong, tanned bicep. *I've spent only one day here, but it feels like I've been here all my life,* she mused dreamily. *I can't believe how reckless I've been—kissing someone I barely know for hours. But I'm not even worried.*

Nina reached up to smooth back a stray lock of hair that had fallen in Stu's eyes. Stu grinned at her and got to his feet to put more stones around the bonfire and pack the sand tighter. Then he paused and shaded his eyes while he stared out at the water. Nina guessed it was a habit. He was such a devoted surfer, he couldn't help constantly scanning the wave sets.

"Oh, man, look at that! Hey, Nina, check this out!" Stu called out suddenly, gesturing excitedly toward the water.

Nina sat up and squinted at the long, slender dark shape that broke through the waves and rose into the air. Another shape soared up beside the first one. Nina scrambled to her feet. "Are they dolphins?"

"Yeah. I see them all the time, but it's still really cool."

"They're amazing," Nina said. Their arms around each other, she and Stu watched as the dolphins disappeared into the surf, leaving a trail of ripples and foam in their wake. Soon the silvery water turned calm again, and it seemed to melt into the dark blue horizon. Nina sighed contentedly as they returned to the bonfire.

"So tell me more about TubeRiders," Nina suggested, settling comfortably on the blanket. "It blows me away that you could run a multimillion-dollar business and still be such a laid-back guy."

Ever since Stu had told her about the highly successful surfboard company he'd started a few years ago, she was dying to know more about it. *Here I go again,* Nina thought with a self-deprecating grin. *I always want the facts—the hard numbers.*

Stu drew aimless circles in the sand. "It was all an accident, really. I never meant to get rich. I created the TubeRider because I wanted the perfect board for myself. Then some suits with money came along and discovered my board. They made it into this big deal."

"It must be exciting to be so successful."

"What's success? Having a lot of *things* doesn't mean you have anything," Stu said enigmatically.

Nina would normally have argued against such an impractical statement, but Stu's Zen philosophy was starting to make sense to her. "Do you run the business yourself—from here?"

Stu shook his head. "No, I'm letting this

194

other dude handle it in our office in Los Angeles. The day-to-day stuff—that's not for me. Imagine that, huh?" He chuckled, and Nina joined him.

Nina grew quiet, lowering her lashes and studying Stu for a long second. "Well, you've got everything you want. You must be content."

Stu moved closer to Nina and grabbed her hand. He looked directly into her eyes as he stroked her palm with his thumb. "I thought I had everything I wanted—until now."

Nina was stunned by the sudden seriousness of his tone. She licked her dry lips, unable to unlock her gaze from Stu's, unable to speak. Her heart pounded wildly.

"Now that I've found you, Nina. I realize what I've been missing," Stu whispered, still caressing her hand. "You're the person I want to share this with."

Nina closed her eyes. Stu's gaze was too intense to meet.

"OK, everyone," Winston announced to the mob of children closing around his truck. He swiftly closed the back doors, giving the woman in the pink outfit a dirty look. "The rules say I can only block the road for a few minutes, and I've been here much longer than that. So I'll have to move on to the next street. See ya!"

Dashing into the front cab, Winston slammed the doors, ignored the chorus of boos surrounding him, and turned on the ignition. "Sorry, but rules are rules," he called cheerfully, gunning the engine. He threw the truck in gear and put the pedal to the metal.

As he peeled out, kids jumped out of the truck's path this way and that, terrified. He heard the woman in hot pink yell something that included the word *lawsuit*.

In horror Winston slapped his palm against his forehead. The truck lurched wildly to the side. "Egbert, you are *such* an *idiot!* You had to make sure the kids were cleared *out of the way* before you drove off!"

Sweat dripped into Winston's eyes, and he blinked frantically. He was about two blocks away from the scene when he realized that something was wailing in his ear.

I can still hear those kids, he thought. *So loud that they almost sound like . . .* Winston's eyes widened when he saw flashing red and blue lights reflected in his side mirror. *Like a police siren!*

His pulse roaring in his ears, Winston immediately pulled over to the curb. *I'm in trouble now,* he thought. *Big, Egbert-size trouble!* He wiped his face on his sleeve and waited.

A tall, square-jawed policeman came over

and peered through the open window of the truck. "Could you step outside, please," he demanded.

Winston opened the truck door, barely missing the policeman with the handle. He put on his most cheerful and oblivious grin. "Sorry, Officer. Is there something wrong?"

The policeman snatched off his sunglasses. "You were driving recklessly, endangering the lives of pedestrians, and speeding in a residential zone. Does that sound like something wrong to you?"

Winston nodded weakly. "You see, Officer. I didn't mean—"

The officer held out his hand. "License and registration, please."

With shaking hands, Winston yanked out his wallet and handed over his driver's license. He prayed the policeman wouldn't ask him to remove his fake mustache in order to ID him.

The policeman's gaze drilled through Winston like sharpened icicles. "I don't see any commercial registration, Mr. Egbert. Come on. Let's take a ride to the station."

This is all happening way too fast, Nina thought, panicking a little. She stared into the bonfire and tried to come up with the right response to Stu's dramatic confession. But words failed her.

I can't handle this now, she told herself. *Not when I'm still trying to deal with Bryan. We haven't even broken up yet—not officially.*

"What's on your mind?" Stu asked, his voice soft and inquisitive.

"Stu, I . . . um, we have to talk."

"Uh-oh. Sounds like bad news."

Nina shook her head. "No, it's not. It's just . . . it's just that I've been involved with someone else, but . . ."

"But what?" Stu asked.

"Well, we're kind of taking a break from each other right now," Nina explained. "I'm still very confused. I don't think I'm ready—"

"Nina." Stu stopped her, cupping her cheek in his hand. "It's cool. Really. I've been there myself."

"I don't want to mislead you."

"You won't."

Stu leaned forward and kissed Nina tenderly. When they broke apart, her lips still tingled. She brought her hand up to her mouth and smiled.

"I'm glad I can tell you these things," Nina said. "And you respect my honesty too. Not many men would."

"Well, I'm stoked that you're willing to open up to me," Stu responded, leaning forward to kiss her forehead. "After that day on the beach—"

"I know." Nina chuckled and shrugged. "I

was pretty stubborn. But I was feeling defensive. Can you blame me?"

Stu shook his head. "I told you then that your spirit was open and embracing. I could tell. You were trying to hide your true self from me, but I could feel it all. This was meant to be, Nina."

Despite the warmth from the bonfire, Nina shivered. "Stu . . . I can't make any promises."

"I know. You don't have to."

"But I don't want you to expect anything of me either," Nina replied honestly. "Last summer I hooked up with this guy Paul, another life-guard. Everything seemed great at the time, but in the end it just wasn't what I wanted. It was just a summer fling, you know—"

"You don't owe me any explanations, Nina," Stu said gently, wrapping his arms around her and holding her close. They watched the sun dip into the western sky for several minutes in silence.

"What about you?" Nina asked. "Isn't there some ex-girlfriend you're trying to escape from out here in the middle of nowhere?

"Not a one."

"You're kidding, right?" Nina demanded. "You must have been in love before."

"Well, yeah, there've been girls I *liked*, but never the real thing." His soft, warm lips covered hers for a long moment. "This is fate, Nina," he insisted when they parted. "You'll see."

Nina put her hands on Stu's broad shoulders. "Remember, I'm not ready to rush into things. I need time."

"I'll give you all the time you need," Stu assured her. "But in the meantime I'll do anything in my power to make you happy."

"How about this," Nina suggested huskily, reaching to pull Stu close for another kiss.

"Ouch!" Elizabeth jerked her head away from her stylist's sharp hairpin. It had just scraped her scalp.

"Sorry," the stylist said through a wad of gum. More carefully she fastened the last curler into Elizabeth's long, silky hair. "But when you told me you were in a rush, I felt a little pressured. I start making mistakes when I'm pressured."

So I noticed, Elizabeth thought dryly as she stared at herself in a giant mirror. The tower of curlers on her head definitely looked lopsided. Elizabeth's eyes drifted upward toward the plaque on the wall, which had the name Misty written on it. *Her name should be Pokey.*

"C'mon, honey, let's get you going," Misty chirped as she guided Elizabeth toward a row of hair dryers. She tucked Elizabeth under a hood, turned on the heat, and sauntered off.

For several minutes Elizabeth flipped disinterestedly through a few fashion magazines she'd found stacked on the table beside her. Before long her scalp felt as if it were burning—especially where it had been scraped with the pin. The back of her neck felt red-hot, and she thought she smelled something burning.

Help! I'm being deep-fried! she wanted to shout, but she doubted anyone would have paid any attention to her. Salome's Salon was totally swamped this afternoon; some stylists were juggling five, six people at a time. Elizabeth chastised herself for begging the receptionist to squeeze her in at the last minute. She was sure her 'do would turn out to be a don't.

The salon was very chic, with pink marble and glass everywhere and silk plants hanging from the ceiling. Hypnotic techno music thumped in the background. *Just because a place looks expensive doesn't mean they know what they're doing,* she thought. Scowling, she touched her hair. It was more than dry; it was sizzling hot to the touch. But unfortunately for Elizabeth, Misty was nowhere in sight.

Biting her lip, Elizabeth looked at her watch. The crystal was a little foggy, but she could still read the time: 5:30. *And I'm supposed to meet*

Ryan at seven, she reminded herself. *It will take me about forty minutes to get to the restaurant and at least twenty minutes to pick up Ryan's gift. And that will* still *be cutting it too close.*

Suddenly Misty walked by, and Elizabeth grabbed the sleeve of her jacket. "Can we finish up before six, please?" she asked worriedly as Misty reached under the hood and felt her curlers. "I really need to get out of here in the next fifteen minutes."

"Too late for that, honey," Misty said. "It's past six already."

Chapter Thirteen

"Whaaat?"

Elizabeth's shrill scream made every head swivel in her direction. There were heads layered with highlighting foils, heads covered in shampoo, and heads with curling irons seemingly stuck in them. Everyone in Salome's Salon turned to look at the blond girl whose face had just turned dead white underneath a lopsided tower of curlers.

"Don't do that!" Misty gasped. "You'll give me a heart attack."

"It's already past *six?*" Elizabeth cried.

Misty huffily pointed across the room at the heart-shaped pink clock over the door to the lobby. She was right; it was nearly ten after six.

Omigosh, I'm already late, Elizabeth thought in a panic. She tapped on the crystal of her watch frantically; it still read 5:30. *My watch died—and today of all days! I'll never make it in time, and I can't buy him a gift either. And now Ryan will think I don't care about his sobriety.*

Elizabeth leaped out from under the dryer and began ripping the curlers from her hair. "I've got to go—now!" she cried, flinging off the plastic smock. "I'm totally late!"

"But I'm not finished," Misty complained.

"Yes, you are." Elizabeth sprinted across the marble floor, her high heels skidding. Savagely she tore out the last few curlers and dropped them as she ran.

"Wait, honey," Misty called after her. "I haven't even spritzed you!"

"Forget it," Elizabeth shot over her shoulder as she raced toward the lobby—and freedom. It was hard for Elizabeth to move in her form-fitting white tank dress, but anxiety lent wings to her feet.

Elizabeth had almost reached the door when the receptionist called out, "Hey, you haven't paid."

Hot tears of frustration filled Elizabeth's eyes. She backtracked to the reception area reluctantly and removed a wad of bills from her handbag. "Here," she spat, slamming the money on the receptionist's counter. "You don't have to count it."

"Yes, I do," the receptionist replied snippily. "Wait here while I ring you up. We get stiffed all the time."

Fuming, Elizabeth tapped her foot as she waited. Her heart broke into more and more pieces with each passing second.

How did I come up with this stupid idea in the first place? she wondered, fighting back tears. *This is the kind of thing Jessica would do. Ryan loves me the way I am. He wouldn't care if I met him at a White House reception with my hair in a ponytail.*

"I owe you five dollars and fifty cents," the receptionist announced, opening her cash register.

"Keep it—that's Misty's tip," she said angrily, her tears beginning to fall. "Even though she doesn't deserve it."

As Elizabeth pushed her way out the door she heard the receptionist call out, "Don't cry, dear. You may not think that style is for you, but our hair designers know best."

Her broken heart racing, Elizabeth ran to the Jeep, threw herself in the driver's seat, and dug through the glove compartment for a scrunchie. When she caught a glimpse of herself in the rearview mirror, she had to stifle a wail. Her head looked as if it was covered in a raggedy, uneven mop.

"No big deal. I can handle this," Elizabeth

said, trying desperately to calm herself down. It took her just seconds to pull her hair back into a perfectly acceptable ponytail. Then she started up the Jeep and peeled out of the parking lot, racing for the freeway.

Please don't be angry, Ryan, Elizabeth begged silently as she sped down the road. *I just wanted to make tonight perfect. I didn't mean to mess things up.* When she flew past a gas station, she thought for a second about using their phone. But calling information and searching for the number of the restaurant would only slow her down more.

Elizabeth pressed down harder on the gas pedal, ignoring the speed limit completely. *I'm coming, Ryan,* she called silently. *Please don't give up on me.*

"Wendy, you saved my life. Thanks a zillion," Winston said dramatically, leaning back against the plush pale blue leather seat of a brand-new Mercedes.

"Hey, what are friends for, Win?" Wendy Wolman Paloma asked, grinning as she carefully maneuvered the big car down the freeway.

Last summer Wendy had been a pleasant-looking but plain girl who shared Winston's taste for mischief. Now she was a married woman who appeared totally elegant and a little intimidating. Tonight Wendy was wearing a designer pantsuit that complimented her long, lean figure. A gigantic emerald shone in an antique-set ring on her right hand. The diamond wedding ring on Wendy's left hand looked big and heavy enough to break her slim finger. *This must be her pick-up-your-buddies-from-jail outfit,* he thought in awe.

Winston felt incredibly lucky that Wendy had been home when he called from the police station. She'd even bailed him out since Winston was short on cash and the police refused to take MasterCard. "Don't worry, Wendy. I'll pay you back as soon as I get my first paycheck."

"*If* you get your first paycheck," Wendy said with a chuckle. She ran a manicured hand through her straight brown hair, which was now layered and styled in what looked like a very expensive cut. "Who knows if your boss will be willing to pay you after this mess. Just don't worry about the money, Winston. *I* sure don't worry about it anymore."

"Easy for you to say, Mrs. Moneybags," Winston joked, leaning back and stretching in his comfy, friendly old SVU sweatpants and Dudley Do-Right T-shirt. Wendy, always on the ball, had brought a change of clothes along to the station.

"Let me tell you," Wendy began, "seeing

you in your Mr. Frost-ee-Freez getup was well worth the price of admission. Especially with your mustache all lopsided and that big chocolate stain on your top hat."

"That job was such a nightmare," Winston intoned. "I'm surprised I lasted as long as I did. It would take a man of steel to survive it."

"A man of steel?" Wendy echoed. "Sorry, I don't think Superman would have lasted. *Lois Lane,* yes, but not Superman."

"Thank you *so* much for the feminist perspective. I get enough of that living in an all-female dorm."

"All-female except for one, of course." Wendy punched him lightly on the shoulder. "You sure know how to liven up a summer, Winston. Things were pretty dull tonight before you called."

"Yeah, it's my pleasure," Winston grumbled. "But don't forget, I still have to show up in court. They weren't satisfied with their pound of flesh. I have to actually talk to a judge too."

"Well, it sounds to me like that woman Mavis is in more trouble than you are."

Winston shook his head. "She can pretend she never checked on my license."

"She *has* to check your license. It's her fault."

"Well, knowing Mavis, she'll find a way to

cover her own rear and let me fend for myself."
He sighed. "Anyway, she can hardly be held responsible for my reckless driving. That's what
got me in trouble in the first place."

"You've got a point there." Wendy turned
down a side street. "Too bad it's not in your
favor."

"It's just not fair, though!" Winston cried,
sitting up straighter in his seat and gesturing
wildly. "I mean, *other* people speed and break
traffic laws all the time. *They* never get caught by
the police. Why me? Why can't *I* ever get away
with anything?"

"Poor, poor Winston."

"Now, if I had been driving a car like *this,*
things would have been a lot different." He ran
his hand over the dashboard.

"Yeah. You'd be trying to get the ice cream
stains off the leather seats. Not an easy task."

"No, seriously, Wendy, what I mean is . . .
you've got it *made,*" Winston explained.
"You're really one of the rich and famous now,
aren't you?"

Wendy rolled her eyes. "Believe me, I'm the
same old Wendy—lover of hot dogs and practical
jokes." She turned up the air-conditioning. "Why
are you suddenly impressed with all this . . . *stuff*?
You've been staying at the house for days."

"I guess I was too stressed out to really

notice it." Winston pushed his glasses back up on his nose. "I saw the mansion, the help, and all the great food—but I really didn't pay attention, you know?"

"That's what I love about you, Winston—you're not like most people. You're in your own little world."

"You make me sound like a space cadet, Wendy."

"Not a space cadet, exactly," Wendy said thoughtfully. "But you *are* one of a kind."

"Thanks . . . I think." Winston sighed. "Still, you must be walking on air. You've got everything you want. Especially Pedro."

There was a moment of silence. Winston shot Wendy a curious look, but she didn't meet his eyes. She drove steadily without saying a word. "You *are* walking on air, aren't you, Wen?"

Wendy kept her eyes on the road. "Maybe we should change the subject."

Winston stared at her. *But Wendy and Pedro are a match made in heaven,* he thought in dismay. *I helped them get together. There can't be anything wrong. They were the most romantic couple since Cinderella and Prince Charming.*

"Wendy, is something going on?" Winston asked, his stomach suddenly feeling queasy.

"I'm filing for a divorce."

"What?"

"I'm not in love with Pedro anymore."

Winston's jaw dropped. "Oh, wow, Wendy, this is serious! What about marriage counseling?"

"Forget it. Pedro's never in town anyway." She tossed back her hair. "Something has to give, Winston, and that something is me. As a matter of fact, I shouldn't be wearing this." Steering with her knee, she casually removed her enormous diamond wedding ring and handed it to Winston. "Here. Hold on to this for me, OK?"

"This place is amazing!" Jessica exclaimed in awe as she looked around the beachfront condo Miranda shared with Theo and Priya. "Everything is so polished and new looking. It's nothing like the creaky old Krebbs place."

"Oh, I like the Krebbs place," Miranda remarked. "It's got character."

"One or two characters too many, if you ask me," Jessica sneered. She was overjoyed to get away from the beach house for the night. Between her encounter with Priya the previous evening and the save Priya stole from her this morning, the Snake Queen probably thought she *owned* the place now. In contrast, the condo was spacious, modern, and best of all, quiet. Neither Priya nor Theo was anywhere to be found; Jessica and Miranda had the entire place to themselves.

"Here's something to wash down all that Mexican food we just scarfed," Miranda said, offering her a glass of iced tea.

"Mmm, thanks." Jessica guzzled it down and sank into one of the cushioned steel chairs in the living room. *Now I can really forget about my horrible day,* she thought, closing her eyes briefly.

"It's so nice to have a little peace and quiet around here," Miranda enthused. "Usually I'm up in my room hiding. I just hate thinking that I'm going to walk to the kitchen and cross *her* path."

"Let's not talk about either one of them," Jessica begged. "Let's not even *think* of them. Why not discuss something more . . . *worthwhile?*"

"Yeah, like that hot outfit you just bought," Miranda chimed in. "Aren't you glad we hit the Shore Mall before dinner?"

Jessica glanced down at her turquoise minidress and matching shoes. The color made her tan seem even deeper. "Absolutely. I deserve a treat even if I can't afford it. But thanks to the magic of plastic . . ."

". . . *play now, pay later,*" they said in unison.

Chuckling, Jessica sipped her tea and was just about to go check out the CD player when she heard something suspicious. *Tell me I'm imagining things*, Jessica thought in icy shock. But the sound of footsteps and keys jingling were real, and they brought Jessica to her feet. She stared at Miranda, the blood draining from her face. "Where's your back door?" she hissed urgently.

"I don't believe this," Miranda muttered, her gaze glued to the front door. "I thought they were going to be out all—"

The door swung open, cutting Miranda off in midsentence. Jessica's ears burned at the sight of Priya and Ben crossing through the doorway. Miranda and Jessica were rooted to the living-room floor, unable to move or speak, like deer caught in headlights.

Chapter Fourteen

"Well, Jessica, I see you're up and around." Priya smirked and tossed her leather backpack onto the nearest chair. "After your little spill, I thought you might have sprained your ankle or something."

"A *spill?*" Jessica cried indignantly. "You have some nerve, Priya. You tripped me on *purpose*—and now Ryan's thinking of firing you."

Maybe he didn't actually say that, but he was thinking it, Jessica added mentally. *I know he was!*

"W-Whaaat?" Priya sputtered, her face turning pale.

Jessica was overjoyed by Priya's reaction. *I can see guilt written all over her face,* she thought. *She's practically admitting she did it! I wish Ryan was here to see this.*

Ben stepped back and examined his girlfriend's face closely. "What's this all about, Pri?" he asked, his voice low and serious.

Jessica put her hands on her hips sassily. "Go ahead, Priya. Tell Ben how desperate you are to make me look bad—so desperate that you'd trip me in the line of duty!"

"She's lying!" Priya insisted. "Jessica's a klutz—you saw how she fell down those stairs last night. She tripped *herself* when she was running for the jetty. If I hadn't taken over, those men might have drowned."

Ben shook his head. "But if *Ryan* thinks you—"

"Ben, you're forgetting that Jessica is a *liar*," Priya interrupted furiously. "Can't you tell she's making that up? Ryan would *never* fire me—I was only doing my job!"

"Oh, sure," Jessica sneered. "Pardon *me*. I had no idea your job was to sabotage your own squad."

"You're pathetic, Jessica." Priya took a step forward menacingly and held her head high, straightening her posture. "You're so jealous, you can't see straight."

"I can see perfectly." Jessica stared down at Priya, stifling a laugh at the petite woman's attempt to meet her toe to toe, nose to nose. "You're terrified that Ben wants me back. You'll

215

do anything to stop him. Like I said, you're desperate."

Priya let out a shrill, phony laugh. "Ben choose *you* over *me*? That's ridiculous—it's as if you're trying to say that Madame de Tourvel should choose Danceny—a total creep—over sweet, adorable Valmont, the music teacher." Priya raked Jessica with a scathing look. "Get real."

"Uh, ex-*cuse* me." Jessica held up her hand. "*Danceny* was the music teacher, Priya, not Valmont."

The argument came to a screeching halt. A stunned silence hung in the air. Everyone gaped at Jessica in total disbelief. Even Miranda was looking at her strangely.

"Ha!" Priya snorted derisively. "I'm surprised, Jessica—I thought you'd learned your lesson last night. Well, get ready for round two because you couldn't *possibly* understand the works of Choderlos de Laclos better than I." She rolled her eyes in exasperation. "I've read *Les Liaisons Dangereuses* in the original French, so don't you dare tell me I'm wrong."

"Well, I've seen *Dangerous Liaisons* starring the original Keanu Reeves," Jessica fired back. "So, yeah, I think I *can* tell you you're wrong."

Priya opened her mouth and gasped. She

looked like a fish that had been washed up on-shore. "Of *all* the *idiotic*—"

"Jessica's right, Priya," Ben interrupted solemnly. "Danceny was the music teacher. Admit it." His face was flushed a deep red; from anger or embarrassment, Jessica couldn't tell.

Priya's eyes widened in horror as she turned to face Ben, her fists clenching. "I won't admit *anything*," she snarled. "Come on, Ben, we're *leaving*." Priya spun around on her heel and strode toward the door. Without another word or glance she threw it open and slammed it sharply behind her.

But Ben remained firmly in place, his blue eyes searching Jessica's. A slight, nostalgic smile flitted across his face for just a moment. "You're a real piece of work, Jessica Wakefield," he murmured, chuckling. "You never cease to amaze me."

Just you wait, Ben Mercer, Jessica said silently, basking in the glow of victory. *You ain't seen nothing yet.*

"How could I let this happen?" Elizabeth wailed as she sped down the freeway. "I can't be late. Not tonight."

Feverishly she brushed away the wild blond hairs that had escaped from her wind-whipped ponytail with the back of her hand. One quick glimpse in the rearview mirror made her grimace; her light coat of mascara was smeared, and her face was blotchy from the potent combination of crying and heavy humidity. Elizabeth could feel drops of sweat beading on the back of her neck, and her dress was clinging to her.

"I'm a disaster," Elizabeth moaned miserably. "This whole night is a disaster."

Through her windshield Elizabeth noticed that the blazing sun had inched a little closer to the horizon. With a desperate groan she pressed down harder on the gas. Since her watch was broken, she had no idea what time it was.

"The radio!" she exclaimed, flipping on the AM band and searching for the first news station she could find. Her stomach clenching, she finally heard an announcer report, *"The time is now six fifty-seven."*

Three whole minutes! She wasn't officially late—not yet!

When she spotted a sign up ahead reading Berriston—10 Miles, she gave a silent cheer. "At least there's hardly any traffic on this road," she muttered. As long as she kept speeding she'd only be five or ten minutes late.

Suddenly the wheel jerked under Elizabeth's hands and the entire Jeep began bucking and straining. "What's going on?" she shrieked, her pulse pounding in her ears as she struggled to hold on to the steering wheel. The Jeep strained to the right and seized up, making an odd choking noise.

"No, no, *no!*" Trembling violently, Elizabeth put on her flashers and guided the Jeep to the side of the road. "*Please* don't do this to me," she wailed. "Please, not *tonight!*"

Something resembling steam began pouring out from under the Jeep's hood. "Is it overheated?" Elizabeth wondered, gently pumping the gas pedal. "Oh, I shouldn't have pushed it so hard. This is all my fault!"

The Jeep was still coasting, but she knew that before long the momentum would run out. She'd never make it all the way to Berriston, let alone the Captain's Feast.

Whimpering softly, Elizabeth was struggling to think of a plan when she finally spotted an exit sign reading Rest Stop about a hundred yards away. Praying silently, she urged the Jeep down the road.

Slowly the rest stop came into view. To her disappointment, it was nothing but a tiny brick rest room and an unpaved lot. Just as Elizabeth reached the gravel entrance the Jeep let out an extraloud wheeze and a powerful shake before it rolled to a halt.

"What now?" Elizabeth asked, defeated, as she put the Jeep in park and jumped out. The rest stop was deserted; there wasn't a soul around to help her. She kicked the gravel in exasperation. As she watched the pebbles fly she caught a glimpse of a beacon of hope on the other side of the rest-room complex.

A fluorescent white light glowed inside a steel-and-glass box.

A phone booth!

"Did you really mean it when you said you'd do *anything* for me?" Nina asked teasingly as she strolled beside Stu. They'd put out the bonfire and were heading back toward Stu's house. Despite the sinking sun and evening breeze, it was stifling and hot. Even the palm trees seemed to be drooping.

"I never say something unless I mean it, mermaid," Stu replied sweetly. "Just tell me what you want."

Now that could be a dangerous proposition, Nina mused. *I might end up saying that I'd like to stay here on SeaMist forever.* She cleared her head of such thoughts and put a finger to her lip. "What I'd really like is something cold to drink. I'm totally dehydrated."

Stu clapped a hand to his forehead. "Oh, man, some host I am! I should have brought a

220

cooler out with us. We were hanging out around that fire for over an hour. You must be totally fried."

Nina chuckled and reached up to pat Stu's arm, her fingers lingering on the tattoo. "Don't worry about it. I was only kidding about being dehydrated. I'm thirsty, but I'm not about to collapse."

Stu grabbed her fingers and kissed them. "I'll go get you some water, OK?"

"You read my mind."

As they walked around to the front of Stu's adobe beach house Nina admired the beautiful wildflowers and lush, leafy plants surrounding it. She followed a row of tiger lilies over to the palm tree where she'd parked her ten-speed. It had fallen over on its side.

"Darn sea breezes," Nina complained as she picked it up. But something seemed different about it. She looked it over and realized the tires were flat.

Nina shook her head and threw the bike over her shoulder, not wanting to damage the rims by rolling it. "How strange," she murmured as she headed over to Stu's front entrance. "I could have sworn those tires were fine when I got here." She leaned the bike against a giant coconut tree and called out Stu's name.

"What is it?" he asked, running out of the beach house with a bottle of water in each hand.

"My tires are flat," Nina explained. "You don't happen to have an air pump, do you?"

"Got one inside," Stu replied. "Here—take your water. I'll go grab it."

"I guess I must have given my bike too hard a workout," she suggested lightheartedly when Stu reappeared. "Your island is awfully remote. Before today I think the farthest I'd ever ridden was across campus and back."

"Maybe you hit some broken glass," Stu offered. "Or some sharp, jagged stones. There are plenty of those around here."

"I think I would have noticed that."

But then again, you were awfully preoccupied, a voice inside Nina's head answered. *You were so lost in your own thoughts, you probably wouldn't have even noticed if the atomic bomb dropped.*

Nina remembered how quickly she and Stu had fallen into each other's arms and flushed hotly. She held the cool water bottle against her cheek and sighed.

Stu hooked up the air nozzle to the front tire and began pumping, the muscles rippling sexily in his lean, tanned back and arms. Nina sipped her water and grinned. His back gleamed with sweat as he continued pumping the tire. Even

222

though she was having a great time watching him, she couldn't help but notice it was taking an unusually long time.

Stu knelt down and felt around the limp tire. He worked the pump a few more times and felt around again. "Here's your problem, Nina," he announced, waving her over. When she reached his side, Stu pointed out a small puncture.

"That's really weird," Nina said, puzzled.

Stu began looking over the back tire. "Hey, this one's even worse." He showed her a long, ragged gash that exposed the metal tire rim. "Yeah, I guess you did hit something sharp. Really sharp. I can patch up these holes for you tomorrow, no problem."

"Thanks," Nina murmured. But she couldn't understand it. How could she have ridden the bike on flat tires? *Who knows? Who cares?* she concluded as Stu stood up and gave her a long, strong consolation kiss. *Stranger things have happened.*

"Thank *goodness!*" Elizabeth sprinted across the parking lot toward the phone booth on the other side of the rest stop. Even though the gravel under her heels and her closely tailored dress slowed down her progress agonizingly, she had seen the light at the end of the tunnel. Things weren't as bleak as she'd thought!

Elizabeth reached the phone booth, breathing heavily, sweat beading on her forehead. *Ryan can come get me,* she reassured herself. *He might be a little upset, but he'll understand when he sees the Jeep. At least I'm only a few short minutes away.*

She dug a quarter out of her purse and tried to push it in the slot, but for some reason the quarter refused to go in. Elizabeth tried again. Still no luck. Biting back a scream of frustration, Elizabeth realized there was a quarter already wedged into the slot.

"Great. Perfect," she muttered, her hands shakily digging into her purse. "I know my phone card is in here somewhere." Finally she found the card and began punching in her code with shaking fingers. Tapping her foot impatiently, she waited for the computerized voice to answer. And waited. And waited. Frowning, she pushed up the volume button but heard nothing.

"Aaaargh!" Elizabeth dropped the receiver in frustration. The action was followed by a loud *thunk*. In shock Elizabeth looked down at the floor of the phone booth. The receiver lay there, helpless.

The cord had been cut.

The phone was dead.

Elizabeth struggled to hold back tears as she

thought of Ryan sitting there at the restaurant all alone, wondering why Elizabeth decided to back out of their big night without a call or a warning.

Maybe he'll think I got in some kind of accident and will come looking for me, Elizabeth hoped weakly. *Maybe he'll drive by here and see my Jeep. Then everything will be OK.*

But in the meantime her outlook was awfully bleak. The bottom line was, she'd promised to meet him at the restaurant on her own and on time. She'd broken her promise. She'd let him down.

Elizabeth leaned against the side of the phone booth and slid down, not caring if her white dress got ruined. She finally sat on the floor, her back against one wall and her feet against the opposite. She pressed her knees to her chest and let the tears fall.

She didn't know how long she'd sat curled up there, weeping; it felt like hours, but the setting sun told her it was more like minutes. As Elizabeth slowly came back to her senses, she began to feel more and more ashamed of herself for acting so weak.

Sitting around crying isn't going to get me anywhere, she realized. *I have to be strong and do something . . . for Ryan's sake.*

Elizabeth wiped her eyes as she got to her

feet, determined. "Please wait for me, Ryan," she pleaded. "I'll make it. I'll get to you somehow."

Stumbling in the gravel, Elizabeth rushed back to the Jeep. But when she jumped inside and turned the key in the ignition, she heard nothing. Nothing but the sound of her own sobs.

"Can you tell me the time?" Ryan asked the bartender. "I think my watch is fast." To his own ears, Ryan's voice sounded strained and far away; it was hard to talk through the big lump that had formed in his throat.

"It's a quarter to eight," the pretty blonde replied, her expression softened by apparent sympathy. "Would you like another iced tea?"

"Um . . . sure," Ryan replied morosely, looking back at his watch. It wasn't fast at all.

Unfortunately for Ryan, the Captain's Feast was so exclusive that the maître d' didn't allow anyone to be seated in the dining area unless the entire party was present. And half of Ryan's party was currently missing in action—for forty-five entire minutes.

He had tried waiting outside in front of the restaurant for a half hour, but the air was so hot and oppressively humid that his crisp white dress shirt became soggy and his dark suit and tie threatened to smother him. In the end he gave up and took a seat at the air-conditioned bar that dominated the restaurant's cramped entrance.

"Excuse me," Ryan blurted as the maître d' passed by. "I'm Ryan Taylor, party of two? My girlfriend is running a little late, and I just wanted to make sure our reservations weren't canceled."

"What time?" the portly man asked.

Ryan's heart sank. "Seven," he mumbled.

The maître d' looked at his watch, chuckled, and shook his head. "I'm sorry, Mr. Taylor. We're fully booked for the evening. If you'd like to continue waiting at the bar, perhaps we'll have a cancellation. I can squeeze you both in then."

"There haven't been any telephone messages for me, have there," Ryan asked without a trace of optimism in his voice.

The maître d' shook his head again. "Just be patient, sir. Something may come up." With a nod the man hurried back to the dining area.

Ryan stared down at his fresh iced tea and loosened his tie. *I hate wearing this monkey suit,* Ryan thought, shifting uncomfortably. He unbuttoned the top button of his dress shirt too, but it did nothing to make him feel better. He still felt as if his circulation—and his breath—were being cut off in his chest. He gazed down at his shiny wing tips. He couldn't remember the last time he'd worn them. They looked strange on his feet.

The bartender passed by and gave Ryan another sad, pitying smile. *Now she's convinced I'm pathetic—and she's probably right,* Ryan thought dejectedly. He scanned the room and saw nothing but smiling, carefree people making jubilant conversation.

They all look like they're celebrating something, Ryan told himself. *I thought I had something to celebrate, but now I'm not so sure.* With that thought his mouth went dry in spite of the iced tea. On the bar lay a single yellow rose he'd picked up on the way to the restaurant. It had long since wilted.

Let's face it, Taylor, he told himself harshly as he stirred three packets of sugar into his tea. *Elizabeth Wakefield is standing you up.* Ryan watched the sugar sink to the bottom of his glass. *But what if something happened to her?* he thought. *Maybe she had an emergency.*

Ryan frowned. He knew that Elizabeth was capable of picking up a phone and calling if she had gotten held up somewhere. Anyone could get to a phone if it was really necessary.

All I wanted to do was take Elizabeth out and celebrate, he reminded himself. *All she had to do was show up—and she couldn't even manage that. I shouldn't have put so much faith in her.*

His eyes burning, Ryan watched the other people at the bar. Everyone looked so content, as if they didn't have a problem in the world. Couples toasted each other and kissed. Old friends argued good-naturedly, each one insisting on picking up the tab. Two young women gestured with beer bottles while they chatted dramatically.

These people aren't letting anything or anyone depress them, Ryan realized. *They're right where they want to be. They're* happy.

Ryan picked up his now sugar-loaded glass and grimaced. *You know, I really hate iced tea,* he decided, pushing the glass away hard. Tea slopped onto the lacquered oak bar. *Maybe I need to lighten up too. Maybe . . .*

Maybe Patti is right.

A new bartender, a thin man with a mustache, had replaced the pretty blonde. "Rough day?" he asked Ryan as he efficiently lined up mixers. "You look like you could use a little something, buddy."

"Yeah, as a matter of fact, I could."

He swooped up Ryan's glass of iced tea and

229

dumped it behind the counter. "So, what's your poison?"

"Give me a whiskey—straight up, no chaser."

"You got it." In one smooth motion the bartender whirled around and picked up a large bottle of smooth, dark whiskey. Ryan was pleased to see the distinctive black label on the bottle—the bartender had picked Ryan's whiskey of choice without even having to ask. Eyebrows raised, the bartender held up the bottle as if to make sure it met with Ryan's approval.

"That's the one," Ryan said, trying to ignore the shakiness in his voice as he watched the bartender neatly pour just the right amount into a short glass.

"Here you go, sir." The bartender laid down a cocktail napkin emblazoned with the restaurant's name and set the glass down on top of it. "I'll put it on your tab."

"Thanks."

Ryan stared down into his whiskey. The overhead track lighting seemed to make the amber liquid shimmer and dance. It looked simply beautiful. When Ryan picked up the glass and held it in his palm, the sensation was familiar and soothing. The weight of the glass was just right, its balance perfect. When he lifted the glass to his lips, the image of Elizabeth

Wakefield's face flashed before him for only a brief moment before he downed the whiskey in one swallow.

BANTAM BOOKS TEMPT YOU TO TURN BACK
TIME AND DISCOVER A SECRET SIDE TO THE
WAKEFIELD TWINS, THE TRUTH! NEVER
COMPLETELY KNOWN BEFORE – UNTIL NOW!

SWEET VALLEY HIGH™

created by Francine Pascal

JESSICA'S SECRET DIARY

Jessica . . . the untold story

Dear Diary,
        I'm leaving home. I can't stand it anymore.
Elizabeth stole the man I love. I've lost everything to her.
I hate being a twin. I hate always being compared to
perfect Elizabeth.
        Only you know, Diary, just how much she's
taken from me. After tonight, I'm not sorry I went behind
Elizabeth's back with Jeffrey French. I'm not sorry about
any of the things I did to her.
        Good-bye, Sweet Valley. From now on Jessica
Wakefield is going to be one of a kind!

Read all about Jessica's agonizing dilemma in this special
edition *featuring classic moments from Sweet Valley High*™
books 30 to 40.

The first volume of Jessica's tantalizing secret diaries.

ISBN: 0 553 40866 6

FANCY A PRIVATE GLIMPSE INTO THE DIARY OF
ANOTHER?
READ ON . . .

SWEET VALLEY HIGH™

created by Francine Pascal

ELIZABETH'S SECRET DIARY

Elizabeth . . . the untold story

Dear Diary,

Todd and I are finished! I've never been more
miserable in my life. It all started when I found a letter on
his desk from a girl in Vermont. It sounded more than
friendly, if you know what I mean. I should trust Todd,
but he didn't make things better by getting mad at me for
being a snoop (as he put it).

I know what you're thinking, Diary. I have no
right to complain. When Todd was gone, I let Nicholas
Morrow kiss me. I even fell in love with Jeffrey French.
But Todd doesn't know the worst. Only you, Diary, know
the true story of what happened between Todd's best
friend, Ken Matthews, and me.

Read all about Elizabeth's steamy affair in this special
edition *featuring classic moments from Sweet Valley High*™
books 20 to 30.

The first volume of Elizabeth's tantalizing secret diaries.

ISBN: 0 553 40927 1

Created by Francine Pascal

Ask your bookseller for any titles you may have missed. The Sweet Valley University series is published by Bantam Books.